THE WILL

BENJAMIN LASKIN

ARETÊ BOOKS

Published by Aretê Books

Cover design by Domi at Inspired Cover Designs

ISBN: 978-1-5005-9658-3

❊ Created with Vellum

For the untapped will in everyone.

1

YEAR ONE

They do me wrong who say I come no more,
Whence once I knock and fail to find you in,
For every day I stand outside your door,
And bid you wake and rise; to fight and win.
—Walter Malone, 'Opportunity'

PENNE FROM HEAVEN

*T*ing.

The garage elevator door slid open. Josh McCain peeked through the massive leaves of a six-foot-tall potted rubber tree plant. Late for work—his shirt half-untucked, his silk tie about his neck like an open noose, and wearing his sports coat with only one arm through its sleeves—Josh snatched up the plant and scooted towards his car.

The rubber tree waving perilously side to side, Josh fumbled for his keys to his yellow Porsche, nearly dropped the plant, and remotely unlocked the door. He opened the sunroof and carefully maneuvered the rubber tree into the car and onto the passenger's seat. He started the Porsche and roared towards the exit booth.

The guard, a hefty, bearded man, hung up the intercom phone. He tugged the brim of his Yankee's baseball cap and turned to the Porsche as it pulled up alongside him.

"Hey, Josh," the guard said, regret in his voice. "Sorry man, but your lady just called saying you're off her visitor's list." He gestured towards the rubber tree poking through the sunroof. "I guess this time it's the real deal, huh?"

"Nah. You know chicks, Nick. It's all about the drama. How much?"

"Thirty-five bucks."

Josh opened the ashtray and pulled out two twenties. "Keep the change."

"I'll hold your parking spot."

"Cool. See you soon, Nick." Josh squealed out of the parking garage.

Minutes later he was hurtling along the turnpike, the rubber tree's leaves flapping and ripping away in the wind. He pushed a button on his dash and said to the autodial, "Kyle."

He heard the phone ring over the speaker and then Kyle's familiar voice, "Aren't you supposed to be at work?"

"Ten minutes ago. Hillman's gonna kill me. But this time it's not my fault."

"Josh, he already knows it never is."

"Where are you?"

"Dude, I told you before, I'm in LA taking depositions. I won't be back till Sunday."

"Right. I forgot."

"What's up? You sound bummed."

"Just motoring down the turnpike with Fluffy."

"What's a Fluffy?"

"The rubber tree Julie and I were going to raise together. Pets weren't allowed in the building, so," Josh patted the tree, "I got us Fluffy here. It grew a lot in a year."

"Ahh," Kyle said, "but you didn't, right? Come on, what else did she say?"

Unaware that the leaves from his rubber tree were flying off with the wind, Josh raised his hand and recounted her charges one failure per digit: "I'm selfish. Irresponsible. Only think about sex. Don't take her seriously enough. Won't ever change…"

"Whoa, hold on. I think I'm having déjà vu."

Josh fished into his shirt pocket and pulled out a ring. He looked at it nostalgically. "She gave me the ring back too."

"You never told me you gave her a ring!"

"I won it from a gum ball machine in Atlantic City."

"A toy ring?"

"What a weekend that was. And man, the sex. We must have done… How come she forgets all the good times, huh?" Josh squirmed and reached into his pants. He pulled out a pasta noodle and held it up, examining it like a rare artifact. "Oh, and she threw penne at me."

"Your thoughts aren't worth a penny."

"Pasta. I promised to cook her a big pasta dinner and never did. Dude, what do I know between oregano and basil?" He heard the tone for call waiting. "Hold on, I got another call. I bet it's Julie. She misses me already." He pushed a button on the console. "Hello…?"

Josh swerved to the emergency lane and screeched to a halt. He stared ahead in shock and disbelief. A big rubber tree leaf wafted onto his windshield. "Dad…" he said, grief-stricken. He dropped his head onto the steering wheel. Fluffy's sole remaining leaf saluted into the breeze.

THE MASTER

"...Taylor McCain possessed a spirit unspoiled by his hard-earned success. More than an industrial pioneer, Taylor McCain was a philosopher and a poet—a man of unshakable faith in himself, and in the goodness of others. I've never met anyone who believed more strongly in the potential of the human spirit than Taylor, and his many accomplishments will surely be felt in his community for a generation to come..."

Father Tillack, a tall, lean man of sixty with a hawkish nose, sloping shoulders, and protruding Adam's apple, lifted his kind, powder-blue eyes, and paused. Before him was a canopy of raised umbrellas in the September drizzle. The ink on the page he was reading from had begun to smear. It was too long anyway, he thought.

He folded the pages and stuffed them into his pocket. Father Tillack conjured up his departed friend in front of him. He smiled to himself thinking how Taylor would forever remain in the memories of his friends as the broad shouldered, ruggedly handsome man of action that they had always known him to be. Brief is better, Father Tillack thought. After all, didn't Taylor once tell him that long-winded people were adored by no one but themselves?

Scanning the assemblage of mourners for familiar faces, he singled out Jeffrey Barnes, Chad Jefferson, and Wayne Powers standing solemnly together. He knew them all to have been Taylor's best friends since their school days, inseparable and fiercely loyal. He figured they must have felt that with Taylor McCain's passing that they had lost their captain. The chic, attractive woman standing beside them, he deduced, must be Taylor's sister, Brooke. He saw the family resemblance in her eyes. Father Tillack searched between the umbrellas for the face that he knew Taylor had cherished the most. Ah, there you are, Josh. Father Tillack continued:

"...What often distinguishes one person from another are one's highest ideals, and the tenacity with which that person adheres to their authority. An admirer of the ancient Greeks, Taylor subscribed to their philosophy of *aretê*, or excellence—a sound mind in a sound body; the mastering of one's inborn capacities; the expressing of the best of one's human nature. Shortly before his untimely but heroic death, Taylor told me that he felt that he himself had shot wide of the mark. He spoke to me of a promise he made to himself; a promise to rectify certain errors and regrets. Had his life not been tragically cut short, I'm sure he'd have done all he could to fulfill that pledge."

Father Tillack set his eyes on Josh. "...But knowing Taylor McCain, even the grave will have a tough time keeping him from the vow he made, for as he always believed, where there's a will there's a way. Convinced that we all deserve a second chance, Taylor McCain never gave up on anything or anyone."

Josh noted his father's three friends nodding at him, as if in confirmation of the priest's words. He was tempted to roll his eyes. Maybe he already had, out of habit? *Did I...? Shit*. Someone handed him a shovel. He looked contemplatively into the grave, scooped a shovelful of dirt onto the casket, and passed it on.

Later, his eyes fixed on his car's vanity mirror, Josh watched a fat tear speed down his cheek. He wiped it away and started his car. A knuckle rapped on the window. Josh quickly slipped on his sunglasses and rolled down the window.

"I thought I'd see our buddy Kyle here," Mr. Barnes said.

"He's stuck in LA taking depositions. He sends his condolences. I'll see him tomorrow."

Barnes nodded. "Don't forget, Josh, ten a.m. at your father's office. And, please, spare us your customary tardiness, okay?"

"Damn, Jeffrey, I'm just entering REM sleep at ten." He grinned mischievously. "Make it twelve and I might be early."

"And pigs fly," Barnes said. He rubbed Josh's head in a display of commiseration. "See you in the morning, Josh."

Josh flashed the three-finger Boy Scout salute, rolled up his window, and drove off.

∾

Still in his funeral suit, and four double gimlets deep, Josh sat alone at the *Cooper Street Bar and Grill*: an upscale pick-up bar, and one of his and Kyle's favorite haunts. To his own amazement, until now he hadn't noticed the two hotties sitting a few barstools down from him. It took the crossing of a pair of shapely legs and an eye-snatching amount of thigh to jerk him from his abstraction. *How long have they been there?*

Josh motioned to the bartender and tapped his finger on his Platinum Visa Card. "A round for the fetching beauties, and another for me."

"Still a sucker for a nice pair of legs, eh Josh?" the bartender said, always desirous to strike up a conversation with a big tipping customer, no matter how inane.

Josh smirked. "Legs reveal a lot about a woman, Kenny-boy. And the less revealing the legs, the less I need to know about her."

"Well then," Ken said, flashing his winning smile and white

teeth, "you must know that lady better than she knows herself." The handsome bartender slapped the counter top in confirmation of his wit, and walked off to handle the order.

With the woman's legs in the corner of his eye, but his mind miles away, Josh drained the remainder of his drink. He toyed with the ice cubes in his glass with his cocktail straw and replayed his father's funeral in his mind.

Ken returned with a fresh gimlet, snapping Josh from his trance. "The ladies request your company," he said.

Josh glanced down the bar. The women smiled. Lady Legs patted the vacant barstool beside her.

"Tell them I'll take a rain check."

"Huh?" Ken said, puzzled. "But the legs...?"

"They tell me she'll be back."

"Playin' it cool, huh?"

Josh downed his drink and signed the bill. "Something like that."

"Right," Ken said with a wink. "I'm taking notes." He leaned in conspiratorially. "So, um, mind if I give her a shot?"

Josh shrugged. "Not at all, Kenster. In fact, while you're taking notes, take this down." He lowered his voice as if he was about to reveal a priceless secret. "Her calves, they tell me that she played tennis in high school, but now she's into aerobics. She skis, but last year she switched to snowboarding. See the nail polish? She's left-handed and her favorite color is pink. She visits a tanning booth, sleeps in silk pajamas, and bumped her shin on her coffee table two days ago while reaching for the remote. When no one else is around, she blasts Abba and dances around her apartment naked."

"Dude, you can read all that? You *are* the master."

"Yes, Grasshopper. What good are eyes if you don't use them to see?"

Josh stood, bowed like a monk, and walked off. Once out of earshot he muttered, "And what good are brains if they're made out of shit?" He chortled and shook his head. "Who you calling a sucker, sucker?"

~

Josh, drunk and disheveled, slogged down the hall to his apartment. He unlocked the door, flicked on the lights, and into view came his swanky, messy abode. Unsheathed CDs and DVDs lay about the plasma TV and stereo, a week of laundry covered the chairs and sofa, modern paintings hung crooked on the walls, and heaped in abandon on the kitchen counter was an assortment of unopened bills, many of them marked 'Urgent.' None of it fazed him. The cleaning lady would be in on Monday and his allowance would be in his bank account on Tuesday. All was copacetic.

Josh kicked the door shut, carelessly threw off his clothes down to his boxers and T-shirt, grabbed a beer, and then proceeded to rummage through his DVD collection. He pulled out a homemade DVD labeled: *Dad's 56th B-day Party*.

He inserted the disc and jumped from scene to scene. He randomly stopped on a segment where his father's friends, Chad Jefferson and Wayne Powers, were standing in a kitchen lighting the candles of a birthday cake. Chad Jefferson asked, "Where's Josh?" "He probably has a date," Powers answered. "Same as last year…"

Josh blinked his welling eyes.

4

X MARKS THE SPOT

*J*osh's cell phone chimed twice, and stopped.

Still on the sofa where he had passed out, Josh looked around disoriented and hungover. He squinted at his phone: 9:45. He leaped up swearing and scrambled to get dressed. In his haste he passed on socks and underwear, jumped into the previous night's suit pants and loafers, threw on a wrinkled, red polo shirt, and bolted out the door.

Speeding towards downtown for his meeting, Josh rehearsed between curses excuses for his tardiness. By the time he pulled up in front of the tall office building that housed the headquarters of McCain Industries, he decided that a simple, albeit sincere-sounding 'sorry' would probably do the job. He glanced at the car's clock, swore again, and slipped into the handicapped parking out front.

On the way in, he got stuck in the turnstile door behind a fragile-looking old man with a cane. Josh gave the door a push and squeezed past the old man, nearly knocking him over. Noticing just in time, he caught and steadied the old-timer.

"Sorry, gramps. You okay?"

The old man nodded, confused.

"You sure? … Okay."

Josh hustled to the elevator, smacked the up arrow, and drummed his thighs until the elevator doors slid open. He rushed inside, hit 30, checked his phone's clock again, frowned, and shrugged in surrender.

"Aw, hell," he said, dismissing the last remnants of guilt from his conscience. "I've been *a lot* later than this before."

The elevator stopped, the doors parted, and in stepped a large Asian-looking man in his mid-thirties wearing jeans and a blue work shirt. Above his shirt pocket was sewn the name, Kazu. The man smiled at Josh, and then began to examine the list of floors on the elevator wall. He frowned, clearly bewildered.

"Whatcha lookin' for, buddy?" Josh asked.

Not understanding, the man waved his hand in embarrassment. Then he got an idea. He reached for his wallet and withdrew his government-issued green card. He showed it to Josh.

"Dude, you want the building across the street."

"English little," the man said with a Japanese accent. "More srow, preezu."

Josh pointed and gesticulated. "Government building. Across the street."

The man shrugged apologetically.

"Okay, okay. Just wait." Josh gave the man the thumbs up. He noted his name tag. "Kazoo?"

"Kazu. You?"

"Josh."

Kazu smiled. "Josh-san."

The elevator stopped at the 30th floor. The doors opened, revealing a large metallic sign on the opposite wall: *McCain Industries.*

Josh led Kazu by the elbow to the window. He pointed to the building across the street, and then at Kazu's green card. He flashed the thumbs up again.

Kazu beamed. *"Wakatta! Arigato-gozaimasu!"*

"Sure," Josh said. *"Gotta-go's* back at 'cha."

Kazu bowed. "Sank you, sank you," he said, elated, and stepped back into the elevator.

"No sweat. Take it easy, Kazoo-dude.

As the doors closed Kazu offered Josh a self-conscious thumbs up. "Take easy, Josh-dude!"

Josh chuckled and jogged down the hall to the conference room.

The conference room was spacious and tastefully decorated. A window ran along the length of the back wall, and gleaming in the sunlight in the center of the room was a large, oval, mahogany table. Around the table sat Wayne Powers, Chad Jefferson, and Brooke Sievert.

Wayne Powers, dressed neatly in khakis and a black pullover, was a freelance travel writer until he struck it big as the author of a series of bestselling novels about a renegade archeologist who solved murders while he dug for ancient civilizations. Handsome with smooth, pale skin, and raven-black hair and beard, Wayne Powers had become a darling of the television morning show circuit, where he easily dazzled the perky hostesses with tales of far-off places and daring adventures.

Dwarfing the chair next to Mr. Powers sat Chad Jefferson, an African-American artist, welder, and carpenter. His penetrating dark eyes, gray-flecked hair, deep voice, and powerful arms and chest gave him the air of a wise and fearsome Nubian Chieftain.

Rounding the corner from Chad, sat Brooke Sievert, Josh's aunt—urbane, perfectly powdered, and clothed by France's best.

Jeffrey Barnes, an attorney in a white dress shirt with loosened tie and rolled-up sleeves, stood at the window looking down at Josh's illegally parked Porsche, his cell phone to his ear. Lanky, almost concave, with gray temples and a keen, jagged presence, Barnes's demeanor warned that he was not someone to be trifled with.

Chad and Powers were immersed in a game of chess when Chad erupted with a violent sneeze. He turned accusingly to Brooke Sievert. The furls on his forehead stood out like a mountain range.

Brooke said, "How dare you sneeze at a three-hundred dollar bottle of French perfume, Mr. Jefferson."

"Three—! What is it, Brooke? *Eau de Pu-Pu?* Welding fumes smell better."

Josh barged into the room. Everyone checked his watch, followed by eye-rolling disapproval of Josh's tale-telling attire.

"I know, I know," Josh said, throwing his arms up in surrender. "Sorry I'm late."

"Have a seat, Josh," Jeffrey Barnes said wearily.

Josh sauntered to the head of the table and plopped down in his father's chair, spinning once around before availing himself to the others.

Mr. Barnes tapped a thin stack of documents on the table.

"You needn't bother with the legalese, Jeffrey. I trust you."

"This is your father's will," Barnes said, ignoring Josh's cavalier attitude. "In it he leaves you over one hundred-million dollars." He pushed forward a sheet of paper and a pen.

Josh's jaw unhinged and his hangover vanished. "Wow, that much?" His astonishment wilted, replaced by a frown. "I always told Dad he couldn't take it with him, but this wasn't what I meant." He raised the pen, somewhat uncertain. "X marks the spot?"

Barnes nodded.

Josh reached for the paper, but Barnes pulled it back.

Josh looked up and smirked at the joke.

Barnes shoved the page forward again. Josh reached for the paper, hesitantly at first, then darted his hand forward. But Barnes was quicker, and yanked it back.

Josh noted Chad and Mr. Powers exchange looks of amusement. He chuckled good-naturedly. "You guys love shitting me, don't you?"

"Josh," Barnes said, "you know your father didn't approve of expletives. He believed they were a sign of laziness."

"I wish Dad was around to still care, Jeffrey, you know, but he isn't."

"Actually," Jeffrey Barnes replied, "you'll be surprised how much your father still cares."

"Huh?"

Barnes nodded to Wayne Powers, who rose to his feet. In his hand was a neatly typed sheet of paper. Powers gave it an attention-grabbing snap. He walked as he read, suiting his theatrical inclinations.

"Joshua McCain has two years to fulfill the following demands if he is to inherit his portion of my estate. Fail—"

"Excuse me?" Josh said, more puzzled than stunned.

Powers ignored him. "Failure to comply with any point will constitute forfeiture of his inheritance, whereby on September 14th, two years from today, his portion will go...elsewhere. One—"

5

HAMMERED

*J*osh sniggered. "Still shitting me, right?"

"*One*," Powers repeated. "Joshua McCain must cease the use of all obscenities."

"Ohh-kay," Josh said with new alacrity, deciding to play along with the prank. "I see where this is going."

Amused, he laced his fingers behind his head and leaned back in his chair.

Mr. Powers continued. "Two. He must read the list of fifty books compiled by me and my three friends before him." He waved a second sheet and dropped it in front of Josh.

Josh grinned. "Dad never did appreciate my comic book collection. It's big business these days, you know."

"Three," Powers said. "He must become proficient in a foreign language."

"*Merde,*" Josh joked. He looked for a crack in the others' stony faces, but to his increasing discomfort, he saw none.

"Four. He must beat Chad Jefferson in chess."

Chad smiled and waggled a white knight in the air. Josh rolled his eyes.

Mr. Powers continued: "Five, six, seven, eight. He must run a mile in under five minutes. Do 150 pushups in a row, 30 pull-ups, and 200 sit-ups."

Josh snickered. "There's that 'D' in gym class coming back to bite me in the ass," he said to no response. The deadpan looks were starting to get to him.

"Nine. He must learn to play a musical instrument *and* perform it in front of an audience."

"The electric guitar I nagged on for but never played?"

Mr. Powers read on: "Ten, eleven, twelve. He must teach something useful, undo a wrong, and finish a project worth starting. Thirteen. He must regularly attend a religious service of his choice. Fourteen—"

"Whoa!" Josh said. "I'm still figuring out number ten. How many points are there?"

Mr. Powers set the list down in front of Josh. "Twenty-eight. You can read the remaining demands at your leisure."

Josh looked around at the inscrutable faces.

"This is for real?" Josh blurted.

The men nodded.

Josh snatched up the list, crumpled it into a ball, and fired it at Powers, who caught it. "Dad wouldn't do this to me. It's my money, and I'm not going through any damn boot camp to get it!"

"Your father figured you'd be upset," Barnes said, "so he offered you a second deal."

"What's behind door number two, Jeffrey? Finish college? Join the Peace Corps? Coach a Little League team? This is ridiculous!"

Barnes said, "Two-hundred thousand dollars. Today if you like. But that's all you would ever see. The rest of your share would go to your Aunt Brooke."

"Brooke!" Josh said, appalled. "How'd she earn his good graces? She's done nothing but sponge off Dad her whole life!"

"She's his only other living relative besides you," Barnes replied.

Brooke said, "I loved my brother very much, Josh."

"Bull, Brooke. You loved his success. Where were you when he needed you most? When Mom died, you were nowhere to be found."

"Your father didn't leave a list for me, Joshua," she replied coolly. "Clearly, it was you who disappointed him, not me."

Josh pounded his fist on the table and stood up. "You'll be hearing from my lawyer!"

Mr. Barnes smiled and wagged his pen. "Um, Josh, that would be me."

"You're not the only lawyer in town," Josh snarled.

Barnes said, "As your dad liked to remind us all, time is precious. Son, the best counsel you have is built into this list."

Powers tossed the crumpled paper back to Josh.

Josh held up the wadded ball. "You call this counseling? I call it revenge!" He stomped to the door.

"Hold on, Josh," Powers called after him. "There's more."

Josh turned. "More?" he said, incredulous.

Jeffrey Barnes said, "Your father instructed me to withdraw from your possession everything for which he was a cosignatory —effective immediately."

"Oh, come on!"

"Your cell phone, your credit cards, your car, your apartment—"

"You can't do that!"

"Already did," Barnes said.

Josh turned pleadingly to Chad. "Chad, he's joking right?"

Chad shook his head. "Nope."

"My *apartment*? Where the hell am I supposed to live?"

Chad flipped Josh a key. "My old place, trusty Schwinn bicycle and all."

"That dump? What about my stuff?"

Chad said, "You've got till tomorrow morning to grab what you want from your place. How you get it over to my place is your problem. Keep in mind it isn't very big. The first month is free, and then it's four hundred bucks due on the fifteenth. A day late, and I toss your ass on the street."

Josh stared at Chad in devastation. He stammered and sputtered, and not knowing what else to do, hammered the wall with the heel of his fist as he stormed out of the room.

Jeffrey Barnes walked to the window and looked down at the street below. "Think he'll be back?"

Chad gave the knight a thoughtful twirl. "The kid is as stubborn as his old man."

"I love the boy too, Chad," Wayne Powers said. "But let's admit it, there's a big difference between stubborn and pigheaded. Taylor was stubborn in his beliefs; Josh doesn't believe in anything."

"Sorry to interrupt the gabfest, fellas," Brooke Sievert said, "but just how will you know if Josh adheres to all these punishments?"

Chad said, "They aren't punishments, Brooke."

"What else could you possibly call such a vindictive list, Chad?"

"Taylor called it tough love. Enlightenment with a hammer."

Brooke snorted. "My ever-prosaic brother and his noble soul attempting to rectify in death his one failure in life." She shook her head at their naiveté. "Gentlemen, we all know that Josh never finishes anything but his beer. Talk about a leap of faith! And you haven't answered my question. How—?

Powers said, "I'll keep tabs on the boy, for starters. He has to complete every item, and many he couldn't possibly accomplish for some time."

"Josh is right about one thing," Brooke submitted. "Taylor was good at making money, but he knew nothing about enjoying it." She held up her diamond-ringed finger and caught the late morning sun in its fifty-eight faceted prism. "Luckily, I don't have that problem."

Standing by the window, Jeffrey Barnes observed Josh storm from the building. He waved the others over for a look. They watched as a man in a wheelchair pointed down the street. He was laughing and applauding. The friends saw Josh look on in dismay as his Porsche rounded a corner at the back of a tow truck. Josh stomped, swung at the air, and let loose what his onlookers imagined was a fiery salvo of curses.

Barnes, Powers, and Jefferson exchanged knowing glances: Taylor McCain's will was in play. Brooke's smirk had no such supernal connotations; her thoughts revolved around a pricey chalet in the French Riviera that her realtor had e-mailed her about the day before.

6

GI SCHMO

*K*yle Dressler, a wispy-haired, twenty-seven-year-old attorney and Josh's best friend, sat at the counter of the *Cooper Street Bar and Grill*. He had come straight from the airport as planned. Josh was late, but that was something Kyle had stopped complaining about long ago. Instead, he learned to always have a book with him.

Kyle was placidly enjoying a tall, dark glass of microbrewed beer and the final pages of the latest John Grisham novel when two-overstuffed suitcases dropped with a *thud* beside him. Kyle noted the luggage with a dispassionate eye, and then with equal indifference, his perspiring and chest-heaving friend, Josh.

Kyle returned his eyes to his book. "Going camping?" he quipped.

"Dude," Josh gasped.

"Yeah?"

"Dude."

"You said that already."

"Kyle, man," Josh said, collapsing onto a barstool. He grabbed a wad of napkins and wiped his brow, "you won't fucking believe—"

"You're wrong. Whatever it is, I will not only believe it, I'll most likely really enjoy believing it."

Josh waved the bartender over, slapped a credit card on the counter and said, "Two of what he's drinking."

The bartender took the card and walked off as Josh began recapping his day in staccato. He had barely tied two events together when the bartender returned waving Josh's card. "Sorry, man. No good."

"Shit." Josh fished out two more cards, a *Diners* and an *American Express*. He handed them to the bartender. "Try these."

The bartender walked off with the cards, ran them both through the scanner and returned shaking his head. "Nope," he said.

Kyle chuckled and turned a page in his book.

"What? Where's Ken?" Josh said demandingly. "He knows me. He knows I'm good for it."

"Ken's in Tahiti."

"Tahiti?! I just saw him here last night. He didn't say anything about going to Tahiti. He'd have said something if he were going to *Tahiti*."

"He probably didn't know yet," the bartender said.

"Huh?"

"Yeah. He called this morning from the airport. Said he met some rich hottie here yesterday and that they really hit it off. You that Josh?"

"Yeah. I'm *that* Josh."

"Ah, well, he said to tell you thanks a million, and that he owes you big time. He called you 'the master.'"

Kyle sniggered and nodded towards the suitcases. "Master of what?"

Josh buried his face in his hands, and groaned. "I'm so screwed."

Kyle put a twenty on the counter. "My buddy needs some beer to cry in." The bartender took the bill and walked off to fetch two more beers.

"Tahiti," Josh said again, shaking his head in disbelief. "That *could* have, no, *should* have, no, *would have* been me going to Tahiti with that babe!"

"Yeah, yeah," Kyle said. "So come on, tell me, what do Barnes and the others want from you?"

Josh slapped the dreaded list onto the bar. "This, if I'm ever to see a dime of Dad's estate."

"This ought to be good," Kyle said. He smoothed the paper out and started reading aloud, snickering as he went. "Pass a First Aid course ... Memorize twenty poems or passages ... Make something old look new again? What's all this?"

"The bucket list from hell. Punishment, Kyle. Payback. What else?"

"Learn to waltz?"

"Remember those movies I treated you to every Saturday when we were kids? Courtesy of the tap dance lessons I never attended."

"Really? What a jerk." He smiled and patted Josh on the back. "But thanks, man." He continued where he left off. "Visit Walden Pond. Hitchhike five hundred miles. Climb Mt. Khatadin? What's that stuff for, getting kicked out of Boy Scouts?"

"Or the zillion hours I spent playing Dungeons and Dragons. Who the hell knows?"

"Learn how to change the oil, battery, belts, and carburetor in a car?"

Josh shrugged. "Maybe for all the times I left Dad the car with an empty gas tank. Shit, Kyle, beats me."

Kyle continued. "Learn a martial art. Learn ten magic tricks. Cook a seven-course—"

Josh snatched back the paper. "It's whacked. How should I know?"

"W-w-wait. Joshua McCain going two years without sex?"

"Powers must have found out that I slept with his daughter."

"Kimberly Powers!" Kyle said, nearly snorting his beer out

his nose. "I can't believe it. You've been holding back on me. But I especially like—number eighteen was it? Knit a sweater?"

"I don't know, Kyle," Josh said, exasperated. "Maybe 'cuz Grandma knitted me slippers every Christmas and I never wore 'em."

Kyle grinned. "I like blue, thanks. But frankly, dude, I don't see you getting past number one. You don't even use words with more than four letters."

"Fornicate thyself. I need a lawyer."

"Don't look at me."

"Why not? You're good. Kick some legal butt. There'd be a lot of money in it for you. *A lot* of money."

"Josh, I'm no match for Jeffrey Barnes. Besides, he's not just the toughest attorney in town; he was your dad's best buddy. Forget it."

"I need money too," Josh said.

"What about the job your dad helped you get a few months back? You make phat for doing next to nothing at that bank."

"I quit."

"Quit?"

"I, ah, didn't think I'd be needing it anymore," Josh muttered.

Kyle shook his head in dismay and pulled out his wallet. "How much?"

"Five grand."

Kyle put his wallet back into his pocket.

"Okay…three."

"I don't have that kind of spare change. Not even close."

"What about *your* phat salary?"

"It's in my phat car, my fat mortgage, and my fiancé's phat engagement ring."

"Oh, right, Kyle is getting hitched. You sure you want to go through with this? I mean Shelly's okay, but—"

"I love her, man."

"How do you know you really love her?"

"Forget it."

"C'mon, I wanna know."

"'Cuz she gets me, warts and all. Because when I'm with her I forget who I've been and think more about who I can become. Someone better."

Josh stared dumbly at Kyle, sipped his beer, and blinked.

Suddenly self-conscious, Kyle added, "'Course, her perfect ass and the unbelievable sex don't hurt either."

"You just proved my long-held dictum—chicks always want to change us. And besides, as far as I'm concerned, there's nothing wrong with your warts that a few beers never cure."

"A guy like you wouldn't understand."

"What's that supposed to mean?"

"I'm saying you put the dick in dictum. Dude, the last thing you ever changed about yourself was your underwear."

Josh grinned. "I don't wear any."

"Just drop it. Shelly's the one and that's all you have to know, okay? And whatever you think, you're coming to our engagement party. It's going to be big. If you forget, I'll be really pissed off."

"When is it again?"

"Christ, you're pathetic. Here..."

Kyle took out a business card and scribbled the day and time onto it and handed it to Josh. Josh stuck the card into his shirt pocket without a glance.

"No excuses," Kyle said.

"I hear you. So, what do you think I should do?"

"First, I'd beg for my job back."

"Let's just say I didn't leave on the best of terms."

"Jeezus, Josh. Then go back to Jeffrey and the guys and try whittling that list down.

"They hate me."

"Shut up. They do not. After your mom died and your dad was on the road half of every week, hell, they practically raised you. You're like a son to them."

Josh waved the list in Kyle's face. "Pain in the ass, you mean. You know they never side with me. If Dad wanted me out of his will, they aren't going to stick me back in. Besides, I got my pride."

"Pride? I see two suitcases and three useless credit cards. And that's all you'd have if I had dumped you back in third grade when you welded the hand of my GI Joe to his crotch with a magnifying glass."

"Yeah, so why are you still here?"

"Beats me, you jerk-off, but maybe it's because every now and then you surprise the hell out of me."

Josh beamed, honored. "I do?"

"I'd have to Heimlich some brain cells to recall, but yeah."

"Like when?" Josh asked, unable to recall a single illustration.

"I don't know… Wait, like that time senior year when you took on Kozlowski for me at that kegger."

"The guy broke my nose."

"Yep, but you put up a hell of a fight and he never hassled me again after that. And it was you of all people who convinced me to stay in law school."

"Me?" Josh said.

"Finals were coming up and I was about to throw in the towel, remember? You blew off a date with Roxxy Salvucci to spend the night talking sense into me."

"Oh yeah…" Josh chuckled. "It wasn't often I was on that side of the lectern." Josh sighed and swigged his beer. "Obviously, Dad couldn't remember *anything* I did right. But why'd he wait till now to dump this on me?"

"He didn't, you dumbass. He tried everything he could think of to get you to grow up, but you never listened. I learned a lot from your dad. Why didn't you?"

"But come on, Kyle, this…" He waved the list under Kyle's nose. "This is impossible. What good does it do him now?"

"Him? Josh, I think it's about you."

Josh wasn't in the mood for self-reflection, and instead explained to Kyle that he had twelve hours to get as much stuff as he could out of his apartment and into the place Chad had offered him. He begged Kyle to help him. Kyle protested, but he knew he was the only person Josh could count on. He agreed after soliciting another promise from Josh that he wouldn't forget his engagement party.

～

It was four in the morning when they stood before room number 7 in the hallway on the second floor of the run-down apartment complex that Josh would be calling home from now on. A flickering fluorescent bulb lit the dingy, musty-smelling hallway. At Josh's feet were his suitcases and a few boxes yet to carry in.

Kyle glanced at his watch. "Damn, Josh. I gotta get up for work in three hours."

"I can handle it from here. Thanks for the hand. I couldn't have gotten all this crap out in time without you. You saved my ass."

"Again."

Kyle punched Josh playfully in the stomach.

"Ow," Josh croaked.

Kyle laughed. "Dude, you're a little pudgy-boy now, aren't you?" He grabbed a chuck of Josh's tire and gave it a tug. "Look at you. That's hilarious." He reached for another flank, but Josh swatted his hand away.

"Cut it out. They're called love handles, you know, and the chicks dig 'em."

Kyle patted Josh's paunch. "Yeah, and what do you call that?"

"My Teddy-belly. Leave me alone."

"Look at you," Kyle said. "You're twenty-six going on Michael Moore."

"Go home already, would ya?"

"Gladly," Kyle said, leaving. "Call me after you're all

settled in."

Josh sighed, and then he remembered something. He hollered after Kyle, "They cut off my damn phone!" He heard Kyle's laughter reverberate down the stairwell.

Josh yanked up the remaining suitcases and slid the last boxes into the one-room apartment with his foot. He kicked the door closed behind him and despairingly noted the sagging bed, faded yellow curtains on the single window, and the ratty, pea-green rug on the badly worn wooden floor. The 'kitchen' consisted of a grimy dual-gas stove, box-sized fridge, sink, card table, and unhinged cupboards.

Because of all the things he and Kyle had brought over—plasma TV, stereo, computer, paintings, clothes, and other possessions he couldn't live without—the apartment felt more cramped than a college dormitory.

Josh set down his bags and checked out the bathroom. It was as dingy as the rest of the apartment. On the wall of the bathroom he saw a "Butt-buster" calendar: a small, daily calendar with a motivational quote to get the day off to a good start. He noticed it was current, and it pissed him off. It read:

Sunday, September 15
The gem cannot be polished without friction, nor man perfected without trials.
— Chinese Proverb

Those bastards, he thought, they were expecting me.

He saw a sheet of paper taped next to the bathroom mirror. One glance and he knew it was another copy of the malicious list. Josh ripped the neatly typed page from the wall, crumpled it into a ball, and fired it at the wastepaper basket.

He missed.

Josh checked his wallet and swore. He had nine dollars.

7

COLLATERAL DAMAGE

*M*oney was the second thought in Josh's mind when he awoke from a long nightmare. His first thought was: Where the *hell* am I?

He sat up and appraised the mound of belongings before him. His nightmare wasn't a nightmare; it was reality. He glanced at Fluffy, the naked, one-leafed rubber tree plant. He had set it beside his bed next to the apartment's sole window.

Josh frowned and reached to stroke Fluffy's stripped skeleton. "Sorry about that, buddy." His eyes landed next on a cardboard box that spoke directly to his second thought. "That's the ticket," he said.

An hour later Josh strolled into a local comic book store, aptly named: *Comic Book Store.*

His cherished box of superhero comics in his arms, Josh proudly set the box on the counter before a rawboned, middle-aged man with a thick, rectangular mustache.

"How much for these babies?" Josh asked ebulliently. "There are a lot of classics in here."

Unimpressed, if not bored, the man pulled out a handful of

torn, dog-eared, and stained comics, and shuddered. Noting the man's horror, Josh's enthusiasm sagged like Superman in the presence of kryptonite. The man picked up one of the comics and attempted to open it, but the pages were stuck together with gum. He shook his head, and with his two index fingers, he pushed the box back across the counter as if it were contaminated.

"Come on," Josh begged, grabbing up another handful of comics from the box. "Some of these have got to be worth something."

The man's eyes tracked an immense dust-bunny as it drifted towards the floor. "In a just world," he said, "they'd be worth a jail sentence." He swept the comics up like a mound of desiccated autumn leaves, and dumped them back into the box.

"Nothing?" Josh said. "Nothing at all?"

Wordlessly, the man slid a single packet of baseball trading cards across the counter, and with his fingers limply waved goodbye.

Josh grimaced, took the packet, and slouched towards the door. He popped the stick of bubble gum into his mouth, and then froze mid-step. He whirled to face the proprietor and waved the baseball card in the air.

"Ichiro!" he exclaimed. "Thanks, man!"

His prized comic books sentenced to an alley dumpster, Josh was not ready to hock anything else, and so he returned to his apartment for a change of plans, and clothes.

Dressed sharply and wanting to make a good impression, Josh went looking for a loan. It took most of the day to be turned down by every bank within a mile radius. Finally, he decided it was a toss up between humble pie and a steady diet of *Cup Noodles*, and so he paid a visit to his old employer.

After being kept waiting for an hour, Josh found himself

across the desk from his ex-boss, Bob Hillman: a fifty-nine-year-old, dome-topped bank manager with an accountant's memory for detail. His ledger-like mind had written off the McCain kid after Josh's first week on the job. He always knew it was only a matter of time before the boy zeroed himself out.

"I didn't expect to see you again so soon, Josh. Your exuberant exit required no encore."

"Yeah, sorry about that…"

Mr. Hillman glanced at Josh's application. "For what are you requesting this loan?"

"Um, home improvements. Odds and ends. Sundries and etceteras…"

"Thirty-thousand dollars worth?"

"I thought I'd be realistic."

"Realistic is what we are looking for. Collateral? Property, securities…?"

"My father's will. I'm set to inherit his estate, but, um, it seems the paperwork will take a little longer than I thought. It's…complicated. But, yes, the will, that's my collateral."

Mr. Hillman looked at Josh's application again. "Your father and I went way back, Josh. We met in this very bank. Like you, he came looking for a loan, a second one in fact, even as he was near to defaulting on the one we had already lent him. Ballsy of him, I thought. But his drive and sincerity were commanding, and we gave him a second chance."

"Cool."

"He lived heroically right up to the end. I have some interesting stories about him. In fact, your father changed my life. Once—"

"Dad had a way of doing that. So, how about it, Bob? Let bygones be bygones? We shake and—"

"I suggest you try elsewhere."

"I've already been to five other banks! Give a guy a break, like you did my dad. I'll pay you back."

"I'm sorry. Now, if you'll excuse me, I have other customers."

"Then how about you give me my old job back? On probation. I swear—"

"Sorry, Josh, but it's not going to happen." Mr. Hillman dismissed him with a welcoming nod to a waiting customer.

Josh got up and watched as a young Asian man dressed in a cheap suit jogged energetically over to Mr. Hillman, a big smile on his eager face.

Mr. Hillman couldn't resist the dig. "Mr. Ngo is here to collect his $500,000 loan."

"What?" Josh said, appalled. "Ho Chi Minh Jr. gets half a million bucks and I can't get a dollar to buy a lottery ticket? The guy looks like he just got off the boat, for Chrissakes."

"You're right," Mr. Hillman said. "About ten years ago. He put himself through college and now needs some cash for his booming software company."

Ngo walked up, beaming. He shook the banker's hand, and in his excitement he shook Josh's as well. Speechless, Josh let his hand be waved like a dishrag.

"Good day, Mr. McCain," Mr. Hillman said, and offered Ngo a seat.

Josh slunk away, his footsteps heavy with the day's failures.

8

A CREATURE OF HABIT

"*Y*ou guys make pickups?"

The pawnshop owner handed Josh his business card. "By appointment, for a fee."

"Just wondering. Thanks."

Josh took a final look at his cherished stereo, and exited the pawnshop counting his money. He stuffed the wad of bills into the pocket of his jeans and walked disconsolately down the street of his blue-collar neighborhood.

Turning a corner he spotted a group of people leaving a bar. The neon lights proclaimed: *Time Out Bar and Grill … Booze … Billiards … Burgers*. Suddenly famished and thirsty, Josh patted the wad of bills in his pocket and felt immediately cheered.

A black sedan pulled up out front of the establishment just as Josh took a stool at the bar. The driver parked on the opposite side of the street and made himself comfortable as he watched Josh eat and drink. An hour and a half later, the sedan followed Josh from the bar to his apartment. The driver of the sedan waited until he saw Josh's silhouette appear in his apartment's window.

Inside, Josh sat glum and shirtless on the edge of his bed. Every sound and eyesore in the apartment seemed magnified. The squeaking bedsprings, whining refrigerator, dripping faucet, bile-green rug, and vomitous curtains all brought home to him the fall from grace that he had suffered.

Until now, many times Josh found himself hoping that the door would burst open, and there would be Jeffrey Barnes and the gang laughing and saying, "Gotcha, didn't we?!" This just couldn't be happening to him. There was simply no way he could live like this for another week, to say nothing about…forever?

Yet, there he was, and there was the sty he lived in, seeping like sewer water into all his senses. *Hum, squeak, plop. Hum, squeak, plop…* The dreary truth of his situation swirled around him like a red tide, and all Josh could do was hang his head and expel a soul-deflating sigh. Staring at the floor he spotted a cockroach scurry between his bare feet from under his bed to the back of the fridge.

Josh growled in a mix of disgust and frustration. He stomped to the bathroom.

In the mirror he caught a glimpse of his shirtless body. He grabbed his flabby flanks and gave them a tug. The size of the handfuls shocked him. He turned and examined his profile, extending his belly even more than it truly was. With a shudder he recalled the comparison Kyle had made of him with a certain celebrity.

Josh shook the disturbing image from his mind and picked up the crumpled list from the floor where it had been sitting since he missed the easy two-footer. He slapped it back on the wall and studied it.

Then he tore off pages of the *Butt-buster Calendar* and caught up to the present. It read:

Sunday, September 25
"The chains of habit are generally too small to be felt until they are too strong to be broken."

— Samuel Johnson

As Josh readied for bed he began channeling his anger and resentment into will. "Tomorrow," he said resolutely.

～

Bzzz…

Josh's eyes flew open. He smacked the alarm, and whimpered. It was 10:00 a.m. Tomorrow had come damn fast. He peeled opened the curtains and recoiled from the bright day outside.

Dressed in shorts, a T-shirt, and running shoes, Josh lumbered down the steps to the street and started a plodding jog. He trudged through the neighborhood into a small park with a grassy common, crisscrossed with tree-lined bicycling trails. He came to a playground and halted under the monkey bars. Two struggling pull-ups and he was spent. He wandered over to the grass and did some half-hearted sit-ups. He was in worse shape than he had ever imagined. Josh fell back onto the grass and stared up at the sky in despair.

From behind a tree, across the common fifty yards off, a camera triggered. Wayne Powers, his telephoto lens trained on Josh, shook his head in amusement.

"Jeezus, Josh, even I can do better than that."

To Josh's own amazement, he continued the routine for two straight weeks. A jog, pull-ups, push-ups, and sit-ups—half-assed though he knew them to be—he managed to get out the door and at least go through the motions. He considered that alone a victory of sorts. Josh also found that it was a lot easier to get out of bed if he didn't get into it with a bladder full of beer, and so he was now dry for five consecutive days. He co̶ remember the last time that he had gone that long without a drink.

The rest of his daily hours were spent with a few random stabs at the list, none of which amounted to much, and to wandering the streets of his neighborhood thinking of a way to avoid finding a job.

Money, however, was a constant concern, and so to postpone the inevitable, Josh paid another four visits to his neighborhood pawnshop. These visits resulted in one benefit—more space in his apartment. Without all the clutter, his dump was a tad less dumpy, and he had to admit that with the new elbowroom the place had some potential.

≈

Josh hit the alarm and opened the curtain to week four. Outside, rain cascaded down the window.

Yes! After all, it wasn't *his* fault it was raining. He felt he had received a reprieve. With a glorious smile on his face he pulled the covers back over his head. Josh's newly activated conscience, however, refused to play dead. After five minutes of tossing and turning, he answered its nagging with a pillow-punching tantrum, and then dragged himself out of bed and to the bathroom. He splashed cold water on his face, and then ripped away yesterday's page from his *Butt-buster Calendar*. Aristotle's counsel greeted him from across the ages:

Tuesday, October 11
"We are what we repeatedly do.
Excellence is not an act but a habit."
— Aristotle

Josh tromped down the steps and started a sluggish jog through the rain. Despite being drenched and cold, the novelty of running in the rain had an invigorating effect on Josh's mood. Plenty of times he had been caught in the rain or inconvenienced by the rain; but he had never surrendered to it before. It felt otherworldly and curiously delightful. The rain had released a number of scents he had never noted until now. He could actually smell the park a block before he arrived there. It enhanced colors too. He noticed that the leaves were greener and the flowers were redder, yellower, and bluer.

He jogged on and his spirits continued to lift. Soaked to the bone he didn't have to care about keeping dry. Whenever he came upon a big puddle he stomped right through it. What did it matter? It was liberating and fun, and for the first time in many weeks Josh laughed. By the time he returned home, the sky had begun to clear, and his spirit continued to enjoy a rare, albeit, short-lived jubilation.

Later that evening Josh sat at his table reading. Again his mind turned to money, and he thought about his buddy, Kyle. Josh knew that if he asked him, Kyle would lend him some money. Sure, he'd have to put up with one of Kyle's annoying lectures, but that was a price he was willing to pay.

Josh wondered how much he should ask for. He calculated that the way he was now spending money he could stretch a grand into four or five weeks, maybe longer if he shopped and ate more wisely and cut out the fast food, snacks, and soda. The revelation startled him. It seemed only yesterday when a grand wouldn't have covered his lifestyle for more than a few days. Would Kyle lend him three grand…?

He yawned and replaced the bookmark; the business card that Kyle had given him.

He froze.

With a sickening feeling Josh picked up the card, flipped it over, and read Kyle's party reminder that he had written the last time they had met. Josh glanced towards the wall calendar.

"Aw, crap."

Kyle was going to kill him. Worse yet, he thought, Kyle wouldn't lend him a dime now.

The truth be told, in the back of his mind Josh knew that the engagement party had been approaching, but he had purposefully ignored the blips across his memory's radar screen. He could have tried explaining to Kyle his reluctance to attend, but it was just easier and more convenient to 'accidentally' forget. He rationalized that Kyle knew him to be incorrigibly lazy and irresponsible, and so screwing up on the party date would just be another "typical" Josh thing to do, right? Such was one of the luxuries of low expectations. But this wasn't something as ordinary as a Super Bowl party, or even a birthday party. This was his best friend's engagement party, for Chrissakes. Kyle would never excuse him for that big of a blunder.

Disgusted with himself for having missed Kyle's party, but even more so for having blown any chance for a loan, Josh grabbed his wallet and keys, and left. He needed a drink.

Josh sat alone at the *Time Out Bar and Grill* and marveled at how he could have felt so good in the morning and then so rotten by evening. He wondered if his life was always going to be so volatile and fickle. Three shots of tequila and two more beers availed no answers.

Outside sat the black sedan, and inside the sedan sat someone wondering nearly the same thing.

The following day, Josh managed to keep his morning ritual alive, though just barely. He was badly hungover, but some automaton within shoved him out of bed and into his damp sneakers. He slogged through the streets, across the park and then over to the local high school where he jogged twice around its track before throwing up in the long jump pit.

Wayne Powers observed Josh's Technicolor yawn through his telephoto lens. Powers recoiled from the sight, and jotted in his notebook. When he zoomed in again, Josh was still retching.

In spite of how lousy he felt, Josh was weirdly intrigued, even impressed by the inner robot that had dragged him out the door while in such a miserable condition. He knew how easily bad habits came to him, but it had not occurred to him until that day that good habits, though harder to form, also had a mechanism.

Josh continued to muse: If thoughts could become actions, and actions could become habit, what, then, did habit lead to? The word 'character' came to mind. And from there it was only a skip and a jump to a line of Ralph Waldo Emerson's from the *Butt-buster Calendar* that he had recently read. "A man's character is his fate," wrote the sage.

Josh felt that some recipe for success had just fluttered down from the heavens and settled in his mind: Thought led to action; action to habit; habit to character; and character to...fate? It was a lot to take in with a hangover, but Josh suspected he was onto something.

9

_____

BOOKWORM

*T*he following morning Josh ripped off another sheet from the calendar and read:

Tuesday, October 25

"Books are the carriers of civilization. Without books, history is silent, literature dumb, science crippled, thought and speculation at a standstill."
— Henry David Thoreau

Books. He had to read books. Fifty of them. He had read maybe five since he quit college about the same number of years ago; best-selling thrillers on beaches in Miami and Jamaica, and poolside in Las Vegas. He knew it would take a long time to read fifty books, but at least it was something on the damn list that he knew how to do.

He went back into the other room and dug the reading list out of his pants pocket. He also made a mental note that it was time to do some laundry. He ironed out the page with the palm of his hand, and took a gander at what he was up against:

1. The Bible
2. *Encheiridion* by Epictetus

3. *Nicomachean Ethics* by Aristotle
4. *Consolation of Philosophy* by Boethius
5. *Modern Times* by Paul Johnson
6. *Meditations* by Marcus Aurelius
7. *Ethics* by Baruch Spinoza
8. *The History of Philosophy* by Will Durant
9. *Essays, 1st and 2nd Series* by Ralph Waldo Emerson
10. *Walden* by Henry David Thoreau
11. *Leaves of Grass* by Walt Whitman
12. *The Law* by Frédéric Bastiat
13. *Tao Te Ching* by Lao Tzu
14. *The Razor's Edge* by Somerset Maugham
15. *The True Believer* by Eric Hoffer
16. *Man's Search for Meaning* by Victor Frankl
17. *Atlas Shrugged* by Ayn Rand
18. *Pensées* by Blaise Pascal
19. *Autobiography by John Stuart Mill*
20. *1984* by George Orwell
21. *Collected Essays* by George Orwell
22. *State of Fear* by Michael Crichton
23. *Democracy in America* by Alexis de Tocqueville
24. *Tom Sawyer* by Mark Twain
25. *Autobiography and Other Writings* by Benjamin Franklin
26. *Up from Slavery* by Booker T. Washington
27. *My Bondage and My Freedom* by Frederick Douglas
28. *The Diary of a Young Girl* by Anne Frank
29. The U.S. Constitution
30. *The Abolition of Man* by C. S. Lewis

"Holy crap," Josh said, not bothering to read the entire list. *And I bet they're big, fat mothers too!*

The list was a compilation put together by his father, Barnes, Powers, and Chad Jefferson, and was in no particular order. Taylor McCain had asked each of his friends to make a list of twenty-five books that had influenced them the most, and from their lists they chose fifty. Having been best friends for most of their lives, and so also having shared dozens and dozens of books over the years, they were not surprised to learn that each of the four lists contained many of the same titles. As for Josh, except for the Bible and a handful of others, he had never heard of these books or their authors.

Josh had nothing against reading; he just never had anything for it. There was always something better to do—usually curvaceous, long-leggy things that involved alcohol and a bed. His father had a large library, and he often suggested this or that book to Josh, but Josh couldn't be bothered. Taylor McCain had a number of honorary degrees from prestigious universities, but he never attended college himself. He wanted to go, but things didn't work out that way. It didn't stop him from reading, however, and there was hardly a subject that he couldn't converse intelligently upon, as his three college-bred buddies knew well.

Apparently, the fruit fell far from the tree, and Josh never shared his father's enthusiasm for books. Josh figured the book list was his father's spite, but his figuring didn't jibe with the dad he knew—Taylor McCain was not a spiteful man.

And yet, what else could the damn thing mean? It didn't yet occur to Josh that perhaps it wasn't about the list of books, but what the books contained.

Whatever his father meant by it, Josh knew that he had better get cracking. He had to read about a book every two weeks, and God only knew how frickin' fat some of them might be. He recalled seeing a used bookstore on his morning runs, and so he hopped on Chad's Schwinn and went to see what books he might find there.

～

The man in the black sedan sat parked across the street from *Shakespeare's Used Books*, which, as the name suggested, was a small, used bookstore in Josh's blue-collar neighborhood. The man had his cell phone to his ear. Through the store window he observed Josh pay for a stack of used books.

"Yeah," the man said. "I see him. Get ready... Go."

When Josh exited the store, Brooke Sievert swung around the corner and nearly collided with him.

"Josh!" she exclaimed. "What a nice surprise." She noted his bag of books. "Aren't you the little bookworm." Brooke helped herself to a peek. "Marcus Aurelius ... Pascal ... William James—"

Josh yanked the bag from her prying eyes. "What are you doing in this part of town?" he asked, suspicious.

Brooke smiled. "Great food knows no boundaries, Josh. Have you never eaten at Saul's Deli around the corner? Perhaps we—"

"Liar. You're spying on me. Well, listen up. I'm going to finish that list. Any other questions?"

"Joshua, dear," Brooke said, "don't blame me for your father's vindictiveness. He left me fifteen percent of his fortune. That's more than enough for me."

"Enough my ass. Like you weren't always hitting him up for money."

"You should talk, Joshua."

"Yeah, well I loved him, and you—"

"And you showed him how much you loved him, how exactly? By quitting everything he ever helped you begin? By a night in the slammer? By forgetting his birthday and Father's Day and every anniversary and award ceremony in between?"

Caught off guard by Brooke's stiletto-like accusations, Josh had no reply. They were true, all of them.

Sensing his defenselessness, Brooke continued her jabs. "You don't really believe that your father intended for you to finish this ridiculous list, do you? After all the grief you put him through, why would he want to leave such a huge sum of money to someone as lazy and irresponsible as you? Your dad worked hard for that money. You think he'd just hand it over to you?"

"Okay, fine, maybe I'm not deserving, but why would he leave it to *you*? You're every bit the ingrate that I am."

"Perhaps he remembered that I looked after our parents when he was too busy with work to do so. Perhaps because he knew I have a deadbeat ex-husband who never pays his alimony. Or, perhaps he knew I wouldn't squander it on beer and women and gambling and fast cars."

"Dad was not the spiteful SOB you make him out to be, Brooke. You might think this way, but he didn't."

"Your scorn for me is quite misplaced, Joshua dear. I'm looking out for you. I'm on your side."

"What are you talking about?"

"It's very simple, Josh. You go to Henry and the others and announce you give up. As stipulated in the will, I will get your share of the money, and then, darling Joshua, your loving and generous Aunt Brooke will give you one third. After all, it's not written anywhere that I can't. The two hundred grand consolation you receive when you quit will cover you until the required two years is up, and then you will be fabulously rich. Brilliant, isn't it? No list. No worries. No living in that dump. You get your money, and the last laugh. Win-win for both of us." Brooke put out her hand. "Shake and it's a done deal."

Josh stared into his aunt's green eyes for a long moment, and then at her waiting hand. It wasn't a matter if he could trust her to give him his share of the money. He could get a lawyer to draw up a contract, just in case. She was right. It was simple, devilishly simple. Why not do it? Just shake and be done with it, *all* of it. His hand rose to meet hers as if by its own volition.

Then he hesitated. It wasn't a voice he heard, but a queer feeling that began in his gut, and then ascended into his mouth. Josh peered at Brooke's crimson nails and the big, sparkling diamond on her finger. A nauseating sensation akin to chewing tin foil overcame him.

His hand dropped to his side. "I can't do that," he said.

Brooke drew back her hand. A sneer flitted across her mouth, but she quickly regained her composure and smiled.

"This is a one time deal, Joshua. Are you sure you don't want to sleep on it? One last night in that dumpy apartment? Or, better yet, you can shake now and spend tonight sleeping at the Hilton."

"I'll think…" He halted. "No."

"Suit yourself. My conscience is clear. I'm not going to stand here and degrade myself by trying to talk you into something so obviously smart. I'm just sorry to see that you failed to inherit even your father's common sense." Brooke's tone turned to one of good sportsmanship. "But, good luck to you! It's going to be a long haul, and you'll need lots of it. Now, I must be going. I have a nail appointment. And by the way," she added, nodding towards the bag of books in his arms, "haven't you ever heard of the library?" She turned and strode off.

Josh watched her departure with agony. He didn't know why he turned her down, and he didn't know why he didn't just drop the bag of musty books and chase after her. He looked around lost and bewildered, almost as if he expected to see his father, like an angel, standing near by. Finally, he sighed and set the books into the basket of his bicycle and pedaled listlessly towards home.

As soon as Brooke turned the corner, she put her cell phone to her ear. She cast a stern eye in the direction of the black sedan.

"Mr. Tweene," she said. "I'm not paying you to window watch. My nephew is showing far too much ambition. Earn your fee or I'll find someone who will."

10

CANDY'S MAN

*J*osh jogged past the pawnshop, stopped, and consulted his wallet. It was that time again.

Unfortunately, except for his plasma TV, he had already pawned almost everything of value that he owned. Vanished were his stereo, DVD player, telephone, fax machine, computer, silk ties, fancy duds, paintings, and nearly every other reminder of his past life, except Fluffy the rubber tree, which, miraculously, was still clinging to life. The pawnbroker insisted that he was paying top dollar, but he was also the only pawnbroker in the neighborhood, and for all Josh's haggling, Josh still felt he was being ripped off.

Josh weighed his Rolex watch, ring, and diamond stud earring in his hand and entered the pawnshop. The proprietor had not become a whit friendlier by Josh's business, and greeted him with his usual smirk and dangling, unlit cigarette between his lips.

Without a word Josh handed over the last of his personality. He calculated that the money he got would carry him like a leaky canoe to the end of the month, at which time he would sink into penury's murky depths. Included in his calculation was one last splurge. And so, later that evening, Josh paid a farewell visit to the *Time Out Bar and Grill*.

～

The bustling sports bar had a long, copper-topped counter and two billiard tables in the center of the bar where some beefy men in blue jeans and rugby shirts engaged in a serious game of pool. Although Halloween had come and gone, the holiday's decorations still decked the bar, including a few carved and sagging pumpkins. Classic rock music rumbled from the jukebox.

Josh sat at the bar, pen in hand. He had decided that if he were going to make any real progress on the list he would have to get organized. The list was too long and time consuming to attack each item individually. With his possessions and money gone, his top priority was getting a job. But it couldn't be just any job. He had to figure out a way to incorporate two or three tasks at a time and still make ends meet. He pulled out the fiendish list, copied a number of the items onto a separate piece of paper, and started circling tasks and drawing lines connecting the circles.

Over his shoulder in the corner of the bar, an attractive woman of twenty-eight with long, walnut-colored hair conversed with an out-of-place-looking, middle-aged man in a beige trench coat. One of the pool-shooting roughs, a big and brawny fellow in a black and white striped rugby shirt joined the conversation.

The man in the trench coat turned to the bruiser. "Remember, Mick," he said, "leave enough of him for Candy here to, ah, resuscitate. Her testimony is more valuable than your muscle."

"Just a little messin' around, right?" Mick said, his voice heavy with jealousy.

Mr. Tweene handed Mick an envelope. "A thousand-buck tale. How it's scripted is up to Candy here." Tweene flashed his camera and telephoto lens from underneath his trench coat and winked at Candy. "Leave the lights on, will ya?" he said, and strolled out of the bar. Candy glanced over at Josh and sized him up with her frolicsome eyes.

The bartender pointed to Josh's near-empty mug, but Josh declined with a wave of his hand. He continued making notes and grouping items from the list together as he searched his imagination for ways to better manage his time. After connecting 'learn Spanish,' 'cooking,' 'work,' and 'meals,' he pocketed the pages with satisfaction.

Josh swiveled around and caught Candy staring at him. She raised a flirtatious eyebrow and jiggled her empty glass. Josh noted the woman's long, athletically lithesome legs, grinned, and ordered her a drink.

Candy sauntered to his side, making sure her hip brushed up against him. She flipped back her hair. "I'm Candy," she said fizzingly.

Josh flashed an impish grin. "Trick or treat?"

"Aren't you naughty," Candy answered, and then added sumptuously, "My tricks are a treat."

Josh scanned the bar for a familiar face. His floppy blond hair and youthful good looks had often made him the recipient of women's advances, and Candy's boldness wasn't anything he hadn't encountered before. On all previous occasions, however, his charm and charisma wasn't shackled by a two-year sex ban. Then again, nobody knew he was there and he recognized no one. He felt sure that Candy's invitation was just reconfirmation that he 'still had it.' The familiar face he was looking for, he realized, was just his pesky conscience.

Josh offered up her drink when a mitt-sized hand swooped in and snatched his wrist in a viselike grip.

"If my lady wants a drink I'll buy it myself. Understand?"

Josh looked up into Mick's cold, intimidating eyes. "Just being neighborly," he said innocently. "You can let go of my wrist now."

Mick clamped down harder and added a little twist. "Just

makin' sure you understand. You look kinda stupid, ya know? Like you've spent too much time in one of them preppy schools."

Josh dismissed the pain and coolly finished his beer. He set the mug on the bar, his hand still gripping the handle. "Actually, I was kicked out of college."

"What for?" Mick said in a pouting baby voice, "Cheating on your home economics final?"

"Nah," Josh said. "…Fighting." He spun and bashed the beer mug against Mick's head. Mick stumbled backwards, but to Josh's frowning dismay, he quickly recovered.

"You stupid fuck!" Mick roared.

He grabbed Josh up like a manikin and tossed him across a pool table to the floor. The jukebox switched songs and boomed Kansas's "Carry on My Wayward Son."

Picking himself off the ground, Josh snatched a carved pumpkin and smashed it over Mick's head. Mick staggered and wiped away the pumpkin innards. Fuming, he charged at Josh like a crazed bull. Josh dodged and threw a flurry of punches but Mick's massive frame absorbed them without flinching. Josh snatched up a pool ball and tried smacking Mick alongside the head. Mick snagged Josh's hand like a first baseman's glove, and shoved him over a table. He yanked Josh up by the shirt collar, and then began to pound him with his colossal fist.

"Mick!" Candy screamed. "Stop. Enough. You're not supposed to—"

"Take it outside, Mick!" the bartender hollered.

Too enraged to care about any plan, Mick dragged Josh outside. The bar's patrons emptied onto the street after him to watch. Mick continued his thrashing. Every time Josh staggered to his feet, Mick threw him back to the ground, and kicked him a few feet further down the street.

Two men in the throng of onlookers were not celebrating Josh's drubbing. Wayne Powers and Mr. Tweene were oblivious of one another. They had never met and knew nothing of their mutual interest in Josh. When Josh spit a mouthful of blood, Powers winced, turned his eyes heavenward, and shrugged helplessly. Tweene shook his head in disappointment. This wasn't what he had in mind. All he needed were a couple of pictures of Josh and Candy shirtless together in a loving embrace and Josh would have been disqualified. Instead, he got a scene, and maybe cops and lawyers.

Powers pulled out his cell phone to call the police. "If you would only put that much spirit into the list, you dumbass," he muttered.

A lone voice bellowed out over the ruckus. *"Yamero!"*

The crowd parted among *oohs* and *ahs* as a husky, unruffled Japanese man boldly entered the arena. Sizable though he was, he made a brow-raising contrast to the hulking and ferocious-looking Mick. Mr. Powers clicked off his phone and watched in interest.

Josh peered up from his fetal position through swollen eyes. "Kazoo…?"

Kazu presented Josh the thumbs up, just like he had in the elevator months earlier. He addressed Mick. "Him my friend."

"Him an asshole," Mick retorted. He kicked Josh in the ribs to make his point. Josh grunted in agony and curled into a ball. Mick pointed a threatening finger at Kazu. *"You* stay out of this!"

"Him my friend," Kazu repeated. "No more, preezu."

Mick strode up and shoved Kazu, but Kazu intercepted his arms and threw Mick deftly to the ground with an aikido move. This impressed the crowd, who expressed their approval with another round of *oohs* and *ahs.* Wanting to see more, they egged Mick on with calls of "Get him, Mick!" and "Kick his ass!"

Mick growled and charged Kazu again. Three lightning fast moves and Mick was half-conscious and groaning on the ground.

Mr. Tweene, his plan foiled by Mick's temper, walked away, angry and disgusted.

Wayne Powers put his cell phone to his ear. "Yeah," he said

into the phone, "we need an ambulance in front of the *Time Out Bar and Grill…*"

Josh squinted past Kazu to the bar's blinking, red neon sign: '*Time Out.*' Kansas's music wafted further and further away.

> "…*Carry on my wayward son. There will be peace when you are done. Lay your weary head to rest. Don't you cry no more…*"

The neon '*Time Out*' shimmied and dissolved along with Josh's consciousness.

11

MUMS THE WORD

Shaving cream covered Josh's face when he blinked into focus the big, brown peepers of Maggie Ardor; a nurse with wavy black hair tied into a bun, rosy lips, and dimples. His eyes darted about the curtain-partitioned hospital room in search of something familiar. They settled upon the razor poised just under his swollen nose. He tried to speak, and winced in pain.

"Good morning," the nurse said, her British accent adding to Josh's confusion. "I'm Maggie, and you're a mess. You've been semi-unconscious for thirty-six hours, have two cracked ribs, multiple contusions, and a broken jaw, which is wired shut. Milkshakes for you!"

"Let me see," Josh said through his wired teeth.

Maggie dabbed away the shaving cream and held a mirror up to his face. Josh barely recognized himself through the cuts, bruises, and swelling.

Maggie pointed at a small cut near his bottom lip. "That one is mine. Sorry. And don't worry, pretty boy, you'll clean up fine in a couple of weeks. Do you remember what happened?"

Josh nodded.

"Watch my finger." She moved her index finger slowly right

51

to left and back again. "Good. Hardheaded, are you? Still, now that you're awake we'll be running some more tests. And then there's paperwork."

Josh nodded.

"Cheer up," she said. "It could have been worse."

Josh shook his head.

"Oh, yes. You could be this poor fellow." Maggie whipped open the curtained partition revealing a man in a head-to-toe body cast, his arms and legs suspended in the air. "Meet your roommate, Mr. Palmer, a truck driver and Harley Davidson enthusiast from Ohio. He's on extended vacation thanks to a whiskey-fueled collision with an uncompromising oak tree. Rest for now, Mr. McCain. I'll check back again a little later."

Maggie smiled, gathered up her shaving kit, and exited the room. Josh noticed that she walked with a pronounced limp.

He lifted the mirror to his face and looked for a clue to who he was, and what had become of him. Getting no answers, he drifted back to sleep.

∾

The flash of a camera woke Josh from a deep dream. He tried to snatch the dream's smoky strands, but they vanished like fleeing demons. Instead, he drew into focus Kyle and his fiancé, Shelly, gazing down at him in wonder and concern. Shelly took Josh's hand in hers.

Kyle said, "Now this is the kind of thing I can help you with. What the *hell* happened?"

"I slipped in the shower."

"Barroom brawl is what your nurse said."

"She called you?"

"You don't remember? In your delirium you told her to call me. I'm touched, Josh." Kyle pulled out pad and pen. "C'mon, this slip and fall lawyer needs some details."

"Forget it. It was my fault."

"I'm sure it was, but you look like pastrami on rye, and there's nothing you could have said to have deserved such a beating."

"I'm sure he doesn't have any money, and neither do I."

"No one should get away with this kind of shit. C'mon, we can kick his ass our way."

"I'm a little tired right now, okay? Maybe you can find the guy who helped me and, well, tell him thanks."

Shelly held up a sports bag. "Here are some of Kyle's things we thought you could use. Pajamas, stuff like that, and I picked you up a toothbrush. Is there anything else we can do for you?"

"Why are you even talking to me?"

Kyle turned to Shelly. "Must be the painkillers." He turned to Josh, "Can you score me some of those?"

Josh said, "I forgot your engagement party, Kyle. You're right, you should have dumped me in the third grade."

Kyle looked at Josh in deliberation. He felt Shelly take his fingers in a mixture of support and forbearance. "I don't kick a man when he's down," he said. Then added with a grin, "Except in court. When I get paid for it. And he can't kick me back. Get some sleep."

He messed Josh's hair to break the tension and Shelly pecked Josh on the forehead. As they were leaving, Kyle paused at the foot of Mr. Palmer's bed.

"What's with the mummy?"

"Motorcycle accident," Josh said.

Kyle pulled a business card from his wallet and stuck it between Mummy Man's toes. Shelly smacked him on the shoulder.

"What?" He flashed Josh an rascally smile as Shelly towed him towards the door by his tie.

12

BRUISED AND LAMBADA'D

*A*ripping curtain and a blast of sunlight flung open Josh's eyes.

"Awake and greet the day, and live as though the eyes of Maggie Ardor were upon thee!"

"Huh?"

Maggie tore back Josh's covers. "C'mon, slugger. We've got tests to run. The first is, can you walk?"

Grimacing and ribs aching, Josh struggled out of bed to his feet. Maggie took his arm and together they hobbled out of the room. As they shuffled down the hallway, Josh again noticed Maggie's limp.

"You okay?" she asked.

"I think so."

Maggie let go of his arm and they continued drifting down the corridor and past the waiting room. Ahead they saw a little girl of six about to enter a room off the hallway. The child spotted Josh, stopped, and stuck her tongue out at him. She scurried giggling into the room.

Maggie chuckled. "She likes you."

"She stuck her tongue out at me."

"You don't know much about women, do you?"

"I know enough not to answer that."

Maggie smiled. "Clever boy."

They arrived at the room where the girl disappeared. Josh noted the sign on the door: DIALYSIS.

"The little girl?" he said, surprised.

"Most dialysis patients are elderly, but yes, kids too."

Through the door's window Josh saw a nurse hook Becky up to a dialysis machine. Maggie tugged on his elbow and they continued their stroll. She noticed that the patients they passed and the occasional groans emanating from some of the rooms drew Josh's attention in a pensive, quizzical way.

"You act as if you've never been in a hospital before," Maggie said.

"Both my parents died in one."

"Oh, I'm sorry."

"My mom when I was seven. A drunk driver ran a red light. A few months back my dad was rushed to one with a stab wound he got saving some kid's life."

"Oh dear, I'm very sorry." They turned a corner and Maggie stopped. "That's enough for today. Good job, Mr. McCain."

"Josh," he corrected. "What's down here?"

"Terminal ward."

"I want to see."

"These people are not dying for your entertainment, Mr. McCain. I have other patients. Time to—"

"I'll find my way."

"Suit yourself."

Maggie hobbled off and Josh continued to meander down the hall. He peeked into an open door. Undetected, he saw a grieving family sitting around a young man hooked up to a life-support system. He was about the same age as Josh, and his mother, tears dribbling down her cheeks, held his hand. Josh looked on reflectively. He folded his arms, suddenly chilly, and eased away from the door. He wandered back towards his room, pausing on his way to peek at the girl on her dialysis machine.

～

Josh spent most of the afternoon lying in bed staring glumly at the ceiling. And that was what he was doing when Kyle returned for another visit.

Josh greeted him by rolling his head languorously to the side and saying, "Forty-nine."

"Bottles of beer on the wall?"

"Perforated tiles on the ceiling."

"Perforated has four syllables, Josh. Maybe that beating rewired your brain. Maybe you're like some sort of idiot savant now. Instead of just an idiot. Cool."

"Kyle, you've got to get me out of here."

"No can do. I ran into your nurse in the hall. She said your tests showed a mild concussion. And you're still pissing blood. Relax, it's nicer here than at that dump Chad is renting you."

"Did you find the guy who helped me?"

"A pizza delivery kid across from the bar recognized him. The guy's name is Kazuhiro Watanabe. He runs a small garage a few blocks away, and get this, in back, a karate *dojo*, which explains how he saved your ass."

"Karate school?"

"Aikido, actually. Nice guy, but speaks hardly any English. A local grad student of his translated. Apparently, the guy was here working for a Japanese trading company when he met the woman of his dreams. He quit his job to pursue his two lifelong passions: cars and aikido."

"Makes you wonder, doesn't it?" Josh said pensively.

"Wonder what?"

"How a single incident can lead to people and places you never thought you'd—"

"Yo, concussion-dude, you're babbling. Listen, I gotta get back to the office. Shelly is going to drop by tomorrow morning. Need anything?"

"Actually, I do." Josh handed Kyle a sheet of paper. "And would you ask her to water Fluffy for me?"

"That stick is still alive?"

"It's in better shape than I am."

Kyle glanced at the paper and arched an eyebrow. "Books? You know, Josh, these don't have any pictures." He smiled, pocketed the paper, and headed for the door.

"I lied, Kyle. I didn't forget."

Kyle stopped.

"I didn't go to your engagement party on purpose. … I'm sorry."

Kyle turned slowly around and squinted at Josh. "Why?" he said bitterly. "Painful flashbacks from my last party when you Lambada'd in my flower garden? I still haven't had a chance to replant it."

"No," Josh muttered, ashamed.

"My *engagement* party, man," Kyle said, exasperated. "My best friend couldn't bother to be there for the biggest day of my life. What, Josh, you didn't think I'd notice? You didn't think everyone there would notice? Instead of telling the guests thanks for coming, I spent half the evening trying to answer, 'Hey, where's Josh? How come Josh isn't here?' It totally sucked, man. *You* suck."

"I know. I'm an ass, okay? I'm sorry. It's just that…that when I thought about all your other friends there—making good, cool jobs, families and all that—I didn't want to face their questions. I didn't want to smile at their stories. I didn't want to lie, and I didn't want to tell the truth."

"Nice try, you selfish bastard." Kyle clenched his teeth and shook his head in disgust. Gathering his composure he said, "You know, Josh, you look pretty sorry covered in cuts and bruises. But in self-pity, dude, you look like shit." Kyle turned and strolled out the room, leaving Josh alone with his conscience.

13

A GOOD SAMPLE

*C*aroline Summers, a white-haired woman of sixty-eight, sat in the hospital waiting room reading to her granddaughter, Becky, from a *Reader's Digest* magazine. Becky's dialysis session was scheduled to start in ten minutes.

Becky listened along, happily sucking on a Tootsie Pop when she spotted Josh limping by, still looking badly mauled. Bored nearly to tears, he was out for a stretch of his legs. Becky stuck her tongue out at him, resulting in a scolding from Ms. Summers.

Josh walked over to the girl and smiled at her. His mouth's wirework drew in Becky's big round eyes like a magnet.

She pointed at his jaw with her Tootsie Pop. "What's wrong with your mouth?"

"It was too big," he answered.

"How big?"

"Big enough to hold my *w-h-o-l-e* foot. What's your name?"

"Becky. And this is my grammy."

"Caroline Summers," the woman said. "Pleased to meet you."

"Josh," he rejoined, and turned to the little girl. "Becky, that's a nice name."

"No, it's not. At school they call me Yechy Becky."

"Who says so?" Josh replied, feigning appalled. "Plain Jane? Simple Suzie? Boring Bobby? I think they are just jealous."

Becky smiled, glad to have found an ally. "Knock, knock," she said.

"Who's there?"

"Howie!"

"Howie who?"

"I'm fine. Howie you!" Becky burst into giggles.

Ms. Summers said to Josh, "Now you've asked for it."

"Knock, knock," Becky said.

"Who's there...?"

Maggie entered Josh's room and found him reading in bed. She spotted the stack of books on Josh's bedside table and arched an eyebrow. He smiled up at her, pleased to see her dimples again. Josh closed the book he was reading, laid it face down on his chest, and pushed up his pajama sleeve.

"Right on time," he said.

"Punctuality is one of the few things in life we can always be right on about." Maggie smiled and set about the routine of taking his pulse and a blood sample.

Josh looked on admiringly. "You're good," he said.

"It's not so difficult."

"That's not what I meant. You're a good person."

"That's not so difficult either."

"Oh, but it is."

"For you, maybe," Maggie said, only half-joking.

"*Especially* for me. But for everyone, I think. Otherwise there would be a lot more nice people around, don't you think?"

"Why are you—?" Maggie picked up Josh's book and noted the title: Marcus Aurelius's *Meditations*. Maggie reined in her surprise. She did not expect the likes of Josh to be reading the Stoics. She set the book back without comment. "There are nice people everywhere. Maybe you just never bothered noticing them."

"I noticed you."

"You were in pain and I'm a nurse. It happens all the time, Mr. McCain." Maggie withdrew a paper cup from her nurse's uniform and slapped it into Josh's hand. "Fill 'er up. We need to see if your kidneys are still out of whack."

Maggie gathered her things and hobbled away in a quick exit.

"Mmph!"

Josh looked over at Mummy Man.

"Mmph!" Mummy Man said again.

Josh got up to investigate. Mummy Man was signaling him with his eyes, wanting something. Josh picked up a plastic water bottle with a straw in it.

No, that wasn't it.

"Mmph...mmph."

Josh continued picking up and putting down items on the man's bedside table and on a set of shelves that served as a closet. Finally he located what Mummy Man was begging after. Josh pulled a pack of cigarettes from the man's leather motor-cycle jacket. He looked around, saw the No Smoking sign, and shrugged. Josh lit a cigarette, and put it to Mummy Man's lips.

Bliss...

14

TOE TO TOE

"'...*Tom* drew an hourglass with a full moon and straw limbs to it and armed the spreading fingers with a big fan. The girl said: 'It's ever so nice — I wish I could draw.' 'It's easy,' whispered Tom, 'I'll learn you.' 'Oh, will you? When?' 'At noon. Do you go home to dinner?' 'I'll stay if you will.' 'Good. What's your name?' 'Becky Thatcher. What's yours?'"

Becky gasped. "Becky! That's me!"

"Yep," Josh said. "I told you it's a great name. Even Tom Sawyer thinks so."

Becky beamed and snuggled under Josh's arm. "Keep reading," she said.

Maggie, undetected at the doorway, observed Josh with folded arms and a disdainful squint in her eyes. "Becky," Maggie spoke up. "It's time."

Becky stood and set her hands on Josh's shoulders. "Promise you'll come back next time and read to me again."

Josh held up his fingers. "Scout's honor."

Becky smiled big as pie and skipped over to Maggie and took her hand. Josh looked for some recognition in Maggie's eyes, but all he detected was mute and glowering mistrust. She turned wordlessly and led Becky away.

Josh turned to Ms. Summers for feedback, but she pretended to be engrossed with her macramé. Josh shrugged and decided to return to his room.

Halfway back, he stopped abruptly, turned, and made his way towards the terminal ward, to the room where he had seen the young man on life support nearly a week earlier. As he was about to peek in, two nurses exited the room wheeling away the life-support system. Josh rushed in, and froze. The room was eerily vacant. He stared in sad silence at the telltale stripped hospital bed. Josh gazed distantly out the window, his mind tangled in abstraction. Finally, he turned and wandered back to his room.

"Mmph," Mummy Man greeted.

Josh grabbed a book and pulled a chair alongside his bed. He lit a cigarette and stuck it between Mummy Man's lips.

"Ever read Walt Whitman, Mummy Man?"

"Mmph."

"Me neither. Maybe some poetry will do us both some good. Ready? Here goes…

> 'Afoot and light-hearted, I take to the open road.
> Healthy, free, the world before me,
> the long brown path before me leading wherever I choose.
> Henceforth I ask not good fortune—
> I myself am good fortune.
> Henceforth I whimper no more, postpone no more, need
>   nothing.
> Strong and content I travel the open road—'"

Josh removed the cigarette from Mummy Man's lips and noticed the man's teary eyes. He reached for a tissue and gently dabbed at them.

"Good stuff, isn't it?" Josh said.

"Mmph."

Josh put the cigarette back to Mummy Man's lips and the man took a drag, his eyes full of gratitude.

Josh heard a woman's voice outside the door, and gulped. "Uh-oh…"

He snatched the cigarette from Mummy Man's lips, doused it in a cup of water, and then stashed the cup under Mummy Man's bed. He hurried to the window, and threw it open; an effort that his cracked ribs made sure he regretted. He tried to fan the room with his arms, but his ribs hurt too much. He climbed grunting into bed just as nurse Maggie entered.

Maggie sniffed the air and looked accusingly at Josh. "What were you doing?"

"Nothing."

"You were smoking."

"No, I wasn't."

Maggie spotted the stashed cup under Mummy Man's bed. She picked it up and shook her head, appalled. "Mr. McCain, that's worse than farting and pointing at the dog."

Josh burst out laughing, which hurt. He held his bruised ribs. "You're funny," he said, wincing, "…and your accent…ouch."

"Enough with your insipid compliments. Smoking is a vulgar habit and I won't stand for it in my hospital."

Josh struggled to stifle his laughter. "Your hospital?"

"As far as you're concerned, yes."

"Okay," he said, "as of this moment, I quit." He held up the scout's sign. "Scout's honor."

"Oh, please, you haven't the will."

"How would you know?" Josh protested.

"There's a difference between willpower and true will," Maggie stated imperially.

"Oh, and how's that?"

"Brute will might pick you up off the floor in a drunken

barroom brawl, Mr. McCain, but that's not true will. That's not what will was made for."

"Go on," Josh said.

"Why, so you can mock me?"

"No, because I'm interested. You've obviously given the subject a lot of thought, and well, that's interesting. Please, go on."

Leery, Maggie cast Josh a scrutinizing eye; then she threw back her shoulders and boldly stated her beliefs. "The will requires direction and discipline. It needs to be educated. And it can't be had in a few days, weeks, or months, nor from any book. Through the education of our will we attain our full range, our—"

"*Aretê?*" Josh said.

"…Yes," Maggie said, stunned. "How is it you—?"

Josh shrugged and answered, "Crossword puzzles?" He nodded to the completed one on his bedside table. "You don't belong to some kooky, New Age cult do you?"

"I knew it," Maggie snipped.

"What? No. Calm down. I'm just saying that nurses, people, don't usually talk like that."

"Like what?"

"You know, philosophy and stuff."

Irked, Maggie said, "Well, you won't have to listen to my 'stuff' any longer, Mr. McCain. You're going home tomorrow. You're free—free to spend your will in whatever debauched way you like."

Maggie slammed the window shut and threw a paper cup onto Josh's lap. She huffed out of the room.

"Mmph," Mummy Man said.

"You can say that again," Josh replied. He turned suddenly to his roommate. "Hey, Mummy Man, I just had a brilliant idea. Can you wiggle your left big toe for 'no,' and your right for 'yes'?"

Mummy Man wiggled his right big toe.

"All right!" Josh exclaimed. Excited, he pulled a chair up to the foot of Mummy Man's bed.

"So, um, let's see... Any lady mummies back in Ohio wondering where you disappeared to...?"

15

BEANS, BOOKS, AND BULLSHEET

*T*he taxi drove off, leaving Josh at the curb gazing up at his apartment window. He slung Kyle's sports bag over his shoulder and trudged up to his apartment. He closed the door behind him and took in the sorry-looking room. A cockroach scurried across the floor. "Miss me?"

Josh withdrew a long itemized hospital bill from his back pocket. He looked at what remained of his prized possessions—his fifty-inch plasma TV—and did some fast math. He sighed in resignation, walked into the bathroom, and contemplated the list on the wall.

~

Recalling a Help Wanted sign from his daily jogs through the neighborhood, Josh went to see if it was still in the window. It was, and it belonged to a small Mexican restaurant with eight booths and a rose-colored Formica counter. When Josh entered, the lunch rush had finished and all the tables needed clearing. After waiting a few minutes, the proprietress, a tiny, Mexican woman in her sixties named Rosa, walked over to interview him. She looked him over, uncertain.

"You don't look like a dishwasher," she said with a Mexican accent.

"What does a dishwasher look like?" Josh asked.

Rosa nodded towards a gangly, pimple-faced youth at the end of the counter scooping some *frijoles* into his mouth with a corn chip. "Like that. Do you speak Spanish? Many customers speak Spanish."

"Not yet," Josh said, and then added confidently, "but I will."

"What's wrong with your face?"

"It showed up at the wrong place at the wrong time."

"Hmm," she said, dubious. "You eat drugs? We don't—"

"Mommy...?" came a deep voice from the kitchen, also with a Mexican accent. Rosa's husband, Alfonso, stepped into the dining area. He was a white-haired, kind-looking bear of a man in a chef's coat and hat. In his hand was an apron.

"Ayy, guy," the man said. He gave Josh a soul-searching once over. "Why does a man like you want to work here?"

"Because you have the best food in town?"

"*Sí, eso es* very true. And, *eso es* very false. Speak naked, guy. I can't understand you."

"Huh? Um, well..." Josh shrugged. *Aw, what the hell.* He confessed: "I've got a lot to learn, little time to do it in, and I need your help."

"You are a strange *hombre*, guy."

"Does that mean you won't hire me?"

Alfonso shook his head in pity. "No, guy. It means no one else will." He tossed Josh the apron.

Rosa said, "Minimum wage, tips, and a meal, okay?"

"Okay."

Rosa sized Josh up again and shook her head in disapproval. "Come early and you can have two meals."

"Thanks!" Josh put on the apron and headed directly to a messy table. He couldn't believe he was actually elated about having gotten a job as a dishwasher. *My God,* he thought, *I've really hit bottom.* A whiff of Alfonso's cooking triggered his salivation glands, and he was suddenly famished. *Two meals? Whoa, that'll save me some bucks!* Bottom could be a lot deeper, he supposed.

After finishing up at the restaurant, Josh went to take care of the next order of business. He cycled over to the public library and applied for a library card. He felt an element of excitement when the librarian, a grave-looking, middle-aged woman with a helmet of red hair, handed him his new library card. He pushed a pile of books forward and the librarian started to scan them.

"The public library," Josh stated endorsingly, "you know, it's a great idea."

"Benjamin Franklin's idea, actually," the librarian said matter-of-factly.

"Look at that. I've had my library card ten seconds and already I've learned something!" He smiled. "How about a computer? Have you one of those I could use?"

"Second floor, by the periodicals."

"Free?" Josh said, amazed.

"Yes."

"Ben-jammin', you were the man! What about tapes, CDs, or MP3s?"

"Sure. Books, music, language courses—"

"Perfect! Man, I can't believe I've never been here before."

"Me neither," said the librarian, not bothering to hide her sarcasm.

Josh tossed his loot into the basket of Chad's Schwinn and dropped it off back at his apartment. Then, he turned right around and left again. He had one more thing to do before calling it a day.

The mechanic's garage was small, but surprisingly tidy. Inside

Josh saw two cars with their hoods up, but no people. "Hello...?" he called out.

He walked around to the back of the garage and saw what looked like a warehouse with big, barn-like doors, which were opened wide. Josh peered inside. He saw a Spartan *dojo* with a floor of *tatami* mats and no furniture, and hanging on one wall, framed black and white pictures of a revered old man with a wispy beard. One picture was a portrait, the others showed the same old man tossing young men twice his size through the air.

Josh recognized Kazu immediately, though he was surprised to see him wearing a skirt. The students, ten of them wearing white judo uniforms, were practicing a new move on one another.

Kazu interrupted and spoke to them in Japanese. *"Jibun no chikara tsukau-n j'nakute, aite no chikara wo tsukau yo! Wakata?"*

Kazu nodded to his senior student to translate, a handsome young man with a strong jaw and serious, dark eyes.

"Sensei says use your opponent's force, not your own. Introduce him into his own stupidity."

The students nodded and continued. Kazu turned and saw Josh, who waved. Kazu broke into a cheery smile and walked over. "Josh-san!" he said. *"Yarareta, ne."*

"Huh?" Josh said.

"Curtis-san," Kazu called out to the senior student, waving him over. Josh figured that the guy was the graduate student that had translated for Kyle. He looked of mixed Asian and Anglo parentage. Kazu spoke to him in Japanese.

"He says you look bad," the student said.

"I'm okay. Tell him I came by to thank him for his help."

Curtis translated and Kazu replied again in Japanese. Curtis said, "Sensei says don't mention it. He says he wishes to be your friend."

"I'd like that," Josh said. "Will you ask him if he's accepting new students?"

Curtis translated. "Sensei says serious students are always welcome."

"I understand. I just started a new job so, um, I was wondering if I could do some work or something around here until I get a paycheck or two."

The student reported Josh's request. Kazu thought for a moment, and then gave his reply. Curtis said, "Sensei is looking for an English teacher. Aikido for English. Deal?"

"Even if I've never taught before?"

The student consulted with Kazu and turned back to Josh. "Sensei thinks you have much *ki* and can do anything you put your mind to."

"*Ki?*"

"Energy," the student explained. "Force, spirit, will."

Josh chuckled, "I don't know about that, but—"

Kazu waved a stern, berating finger. He spoke rapidly to his student and motioned impatiently for a translation.

"Sensei says, lesson one—no doubting. Doubt robs you of your *ki*. *Ki* follows mind. Think so, believe so, do so. In aikido and in life."

"Okay, I'll try."

Kazu shook a censuring finger. "Try is bullsheet!"

"Okay, okay…"

Kazu nodded sternly and returned to his class.

Josh turned to the student. "Wow, for a guy in a skirt he takes this stuff pretty seriously."

Curtis wasn't amused. "It's called a *hakama*. And it looks that way to you because you are ignorant. Sensei says ignorant people think the trivial serious and the serious trivial. He says when you know who you are and what you need, nothing is trivial, and everything is hilariously interesting. Sensei is the least serious man I know."

Afraid he had gotten off on the wrong foot, Josh said, "Anyone ever tell you that you look like Kwai Chang Cain from the TV show *Kung Fu?*"

"Anyone ever tell you that you look like the turd in their toilet?" Curtis rejoined.

"Dude," Josh said, hurt. "Mine was a *compliment*. Cain was cool."

"No, he was an actor."

"Oh, I get it," Josh said. "You're using some of that Zen sound-of-one-hand-clapping stuff on me, aren't you?"

Curtis rolled his eyes. "'Dude,' I don't know what the hell you're talking about. Besides, I'm Jewish." He walked away with a smile.

16

A DAY IN THE LIFE

Monday, December 12

"To live content with small means; to seek elegance rather than luxury, and refinement rather than fashion; to be worthy, not respectable, and wealthy, not, rich; to listen to stars and birds, babes and sages, with open heart; to study hard; to think quietly, act frankly, talk gently, await occasions, hurry never; in a word, to let the spiritual, unbidden and unconscious, grow up through the common—this is my symphony."
— William Henry Channing (1780-1842)

*J*osh strolled into the hospital waiting room and greeted Becky and Ms. Summers with, "Knock, knock."

Becky's face lit up and she ran to meet him. "Who's there?"

"Orange."

"Orange who?"

Josh smiled big and proud, showing off his newly naked teeth. "Orange-ya gonna say I'm handsome?"

Becky shrieked with giggling surprise, and then Josh noticed that something had Ms. Summers' eye. He followed her glance to Maggie standing disapprovingly in the doorway. She walked away. *Man, what's her problem?*

～

Josh finished clearing the last table from the lunch rush. Now, at long last, he had his first chance to try out his newly freed choppers on Alfonso's delicious-smelling cooking. The aroma had been tormenting him for weeks.

"Here, dear," Rosa said. She set down a plate of rice, beans, and enchiladas on the lunch counter. Josh hopped onto a barstool and dove in ravenously.

Between shovelfuls, Josh squealed in ecstasy, "Oh, man! … Oh, baby! Rosa, these beans are amazing!"

"Daddy is the best, dear."

"What's his secret?"

"He meditates over them, dear."

Josh laughed. "What?"

"Oh, yes. Daddy takes beans *very* serious."

Rosa pointed towards a framed certificate on the wall. It read:

PEOPLE'S CHOICE AWARD
"Best Transcendental Mexican Food"
ALFONSO'S MEXICAN FOOD

"Can Alfonso cook anything?" Josh asked.

"*Sí*, dear. He's a *Cordon Bleu* chef. In the Army he prepared meals for two presidents!" She called out to the kitchen, "Didn't you, Daddy?"

"That's right, guy," Alfonso answered.

Josh speared an enchilada with his fork. "Hey, Al. Do you think you could teach me to cook?"

"No, guy," Alfonso answered.

"No? Why not?"

"Preparing food for a person's stomach is a great responsibility."

"So?"

Alfonso emerged from the kitchen stirring a pot. He noted

the dripping enchilada dangling from Josh's mouth. He shook his head. "Pigs can't cook."

❧

Although Josh had been released from the hospital a month already, he knew that Mummy Man was still there in near suspended animation. He felt a soldierly obligation to the guy, and so he continued to visit him for thirty minutes almost every day.

By means of their left-toe, right-toe confabulations, Josh had gotten to know Mummy Man pretty well. He learned that the man was thirty-three years old, single, married once with no kids, played the mandolin, liked baseball, action films, and carrot cake. He married his high school sweetheart, but because he drank too much beer and smoked too much pot she got tired of waiting for him to get his act together, and so she left him for their veterinarian. The next five years were rough, and they culminated in his present condition.

Mummy Man wiggled enough 'yes' and 'no' toes to tell Josh that he was actually grateful for his accident. Months spent on his back without a drink or a joint had brought a new clarity to his head. He had time to think. And to pray. And to think some more. Ironically, having nothing but time, he came to appreciate how short and precious time and life really were.

He was itching, literally, to get out of his cast and start anew. He believed his accident was divine intervention. God didn't get him drunk that fateful night. He did that himself. He did believe, however, that God put that deer in the road he swerved to miss. Did God overdo it? Mummy Man didn't think so. He said he had received plenty of divine nudges and pops on the forehead—cosmic wake-up calls, so to speak—but he had been too thick-headed to heed them. He felt that he had left God no choice, and so—*pow!* That was the story Josh learned from Mummy Man, and it had taken weeks and hundreds of yes-and-no questions for Josh to unravel it.

By now it had become routine for Josh to throw open the window, insert a long straw into a box of juice, and set it by Mummy Man's pillow.

"Change of pace today, Mummy Man," Josh said. "Like Pineapple?"

Mummy Man wiggled his right toe, signaling—'Yes.'

Josh put the straw into Mummy Man's mouth. The coast clear, he closed the door and lit a cigarette.

Mummy Man wiggled his left toe—'No.'

"No?" Josh said, surprised. "Quitting, are you?"

Mummy Man wiggled his right toe.

Josh nodded. "Yeah, why the heck not, eh?"

Josh stashed the cigarette into a cup and pulled up a chair. He held up a thick book.

"Next up, *Moby Dick*. Once we finish this puppy it'll be time for you to get your smoke-free ass back to Ohio and into that rig of yours."

He opened to page one and cleared his throat. "Ready? Here we go. Chapter One. *Call me Ishmael…*"

After visiting the hospital Josh returned home, changed, and went for a run and more attempts at reaching the necessary number of pull-ups, push-ups, and sit-ups. Whenever he was out now, Josh carried an old MP3 player that he had picked up for two bucks at a garage sale. He used it to listen to the audiobooks he could find at the library that matched those on his list: Ayn Rand's *Atlas Shrugged*, Somerset Maugham's *The Razor's Edge*, John Stuart Mill's *Autobiography*, and the poetry of Robert Frost, for starters. He also used it with an old *Hugo Spanish Language Course* that the library carried.

As he struggled with the day's final sit-up, a little dog of decidedly colorful ancestry wandered up and licked his face. Josh fell back in helpless laughter. "Hey, little fella!" The dog barked his comical opinion of Josh and they spent the next fifteen minutes rolling and tussling, and covering themselves with leaves and grass.

~

Josh finished the day with Kazu's English class. Kazu sat at a card table holding a menu that Josh had borrowed from Alfonso's restaurant. Josh, wearing an apron, walked up with a tray and a glass of water. He set down the glass and pulled out a pad and pen.

"Good evening, sir. May I take your order?"

"Tacos."

"Tacos? Just tacos?"

"Tacos, yes."

"No," Josh said. "You ordered tacos last time. Try something different. And don't just say 'tacos.' Say, 'Yes, please. I'd like the enchiladas, or chimichanga, or something like that. Okay?"

Kazu frowned, uncertain.

"Okay," Josh said. "Again, from the top. "Good evening, sir. May I take your order?"

"Enchirada."

"Yes, please." Josh corrected.

"Sank you."

Josh shook his head. "*Thank* you," he enunciated. "*Th, th, Thank you*"

"You welcome."

"You *are* welcome," Josh corrected. "Again, from the beginning: Good evening, sir. May I take your order?"

"Yes, preezu."

"Please. *Pl, pl, pl*-eeze."

"You are welcome," Kazu said.

"Cut," Josh said slicing the air with his hand. "Start over… Good evening, sir. May I take your order?"

"Yes…preeze. Enchirada," Kazu said, having made a great effort.

"Better," Josh said.

"Sank you," Kazu said proudly.

"Enchiladas," Josh repeated. "And would you like anything to drink?"

"Bee-ru."

"Beer," Josh corrected. "Beer, like *ear*, like *hear*," he said, cupping his own ear.

"Bee-ru!" Kazu shouted.

"Cut!"

17

VISITATION RIGHTS

*H*aving finished *Tom Sawyer*, Josh hoped that Becky might want to move on to another book, preferably one on his reading list, perhaps some Jack London, but Becky wouldn't have it. She wanted to hear the whole story a second time. Josh surrendered to her wish and was amazed that indeed she seemed to enjoy the novel equally as much the second time around, if not more so. Josh was reading from it when Maggie entered the waiting room. She noted the contented look on Becky's face. Clearly the girl loved having a playmate like Josh.

"Okay, Becky," Maggie said, contemptuously ignoring Josh. "We're ready for you."

"See you next time, okay?" Josh said, rubbing the top of Becky's head.

Becky nodded happily and skipped to Maggie's side. They left holding hands. Josh gathered his things into his daypack and turned to Ms. Summers.

"Becky and Nurse Ardor seem very close," he remarked.

"They are. Becky has been coming here most of her life, after all."

"How did Ms. Ardor get here, anyway? To America, I mean."

"Just looking for a new life, I suppose. America's shortage of nurses made that relatively simple."

Josh sat down beside Ms. Summers. "Is it just my imagination, or does she not like me visiting Becky?"

"She's grown very fond of you, you know."

"Maggie?"

"Dreamer. Becky. She actually looks forward to coming here now. You're the first real friend she's ever had."

"What about you?"

"I'm her grandmother. I can't give her what you give her."

"What's that?"

"A sense of belonging. The belief that she can be just like the other little girls that she sees."

"Hasn't she any other family?"

"I don't know who the father is, Mr. McCain," she said, a wince passing across her usually stolid face. "No one stepped up to claim her. Becky was born prematurely and the delivery...had complications. My daughter didn't make it." She looked away and said with a quavering voice, "I didn't even know my own daughter was pregnant, Mr. McCain. We-we weren't very close..."

"I'm sorry."

Ms. Summers dabbed at the corners of her eyes with a handkerchief, and regained her composure. "Becky is on a waiting list for a kidney. If the right donor ever comes along, it will be very costly and I don't know how—" She turned to Josh. "Mr. McCain, Becky is not a little doll. She's a child with more obstacles to happiness than most. We'd hate to see her hurt."

"I would never hurt her."

"Not intentionally, I know. But how long before Becky wonders why you have stopped visiting her? You're a handsome young man with your whole life before you. What use have you for a little girl like her?"

"Use? That's—"

"A bad choice of words. But I think you know what I'm getting at."

"Are you and Maggie telling me that I should stop visiting Becky?"

"No, only that you consider deeply that your actions have consequences, and consequences, well, more consequences."

Josh grabbed his daypack and slung it over his shoulder. "Thanks for the vote of confidence. I got stuff to do. See you later." Josh walked to the door.

"Mr. McCain," Ms. Summers called after him. "I'd like to know if I should prepare Becky."

"Prepare her for what?"

"Your, well…departure."

"I'm not going anywhere, got it? And you can tell Ms. Sourpuss that if she doesn't like seeing me around, she should tell me so to my face. She can skulk behind doors and walls with her snotty look all she wants, but it won't stop me from visiting. See you next time."

18

FOUR

Tuesday, April 4

They were pleasant spring days, in which the winter of man's discontent was thawing as well as the earth, and the life that had lain torpid began to stretch itself."

— Henry David Thoreau, *Walden*

*J*osh yawned and rubbed his eyes. He had been at his card table reading about Baruch Spinoza and his *magnum opus*, *Ethics*, in Will Durant's *The Story of Philosophy*. He stretched his arms and legs, wiggled his toes, and cracked his knuckles. He cranked his neck left and right, and then noticed that the wall calendar was three months behind.

He got up and ripped away January, February, and March. He wondered where the time went. Throughout the snowy cold of winter, he had somehow managed to trudge grimly on. The days came one by one, but the weeks passed in clumps; and now, suddenly, spring was in the crouching position like a runner at the mark.

Josh wasn't sure how he felt about the passing time. On the one hand, he didn't give up on the list; something he considered verging on the miraculous. He checked off a number of books, tripled his push-ups, sit-ups, and pull-ups, could now speak scraps of Spanish, and was holding his own in Kazu's *dojo*. On the other hand, his progress was way too slow. He knew that at his current rate he'd be lucky to complete half the list by the two-year deadline.

Josh also recognized that he was barely making ends meet, lived in a pit, and was lonely; situations he saw little hope of changing. Sure, he enjoyed his new friends, especially Kazu, but he also missed his buddy, Kyle.

Josh hadn't spoken to Kyle since their falling-out at the hospital. He was surprised that Kyle hadn't stopped by to see how he was doing; in the old days he would have. Something was different. Maybe Kyle was just sick of him. He considered calling him, but he couldn't screw up the courage. He didn't know what to say. He had apologized already, so what good would another confession do? Besides, he continued, I'm a lousy influence and just hold him back. He's getting married, moving up in the world, and will soon start a family and all the rest. What kind of friendship could I offer? I don't know anything about that stuff...

Realizing that he was about to sink into a swamp of self-pity, he recalled a line from the *Butt-buster Calendar*, something Benjamin Franklin had said: "The best way to cheer yourself up is to cheer someone else up."

Josh left and went to pay a visit to Mummy Man. They were almost halfway through Moby Dick by now, and there was still an hour and a half until the close of visiting hours, so he figured they could put another dent into that tome. Although he had already visited Mummy Man earlier that day, he didn't think his pal would mind.

When Josh entered Mummy Man's room, he found it empty and the bed stripped. His heart sank, and he felt suddenly nauseous.

He recalled the young man in the terminal ward months earlier and the same naked bed. *My God, did Mummy Man take a turn for the worse?* Josh spun to seek a nurse to find out what had happened, but one was standing at the door already.

"Can I help you?" Maggie asked.

"What happened to Mummy Man?" Josh said, clearly upset.

"*Mr. Palmer* is on his way back to Ohio and his rig."

Josh sighed in relief. But he was sad too. "I'll miss the way his toes curled when he laughed," he said.

Maggie gave Josh the fish eye, but let it slide. "He said you might stop by. He asked me to give you this..." She pulled a silver chain from her pocket and handed it to him.

Josh held it up. A silver number '4' dangled from the chain. "Four?"

"He said it was his lucky number. He said he wouldn't be needing it anymore."

"No? Why not?"

"He said meeting you was all the luck he'll ever need."

"He said that?" Josh was stunned.

Maggie smiled. "Yes."

Josh put on the necklace.

"So," Maggie said, "still reading Marcus Aurelius?"

"No."

Maggie smirked. "Gave up, huh?"

"I finished it a long time ago. I'm studying Spinoza now."

"*Spinoza?* He's my fave—" She reigned in her enthusiasm.

Josh grinned. "I kinda thought you might like him. He has much to say about your education of the will."

"So you remember our little conversation? I'm flattered. And is that what you've been busy doing these past many weeks, Mr. McCain? Working on your will?"

"You might say that."

Maggie folded her arms and sized him up. "Well, I hate to admit it, but it looks good on you."

"Really?"

Maggie nodded. "It looks like you've put on some muscle too. Been working out?"

"I stay active, yeah."

"I saw you naked, you know," she said puckishly. "You had a beer belly."

"Yep, but now it's called a six-pack. Check me out..." Josh lifted his shirt and revealed his rippling stomach.

"Nice. Why?"

"'Why?'"

"Who are you trying to impress? Some girl?"

"No... Are *you* impressed?"

"It takes a lot more than a set of abs to impress me, Mr. McCain."

"Yeah, like what?"

"Wouldn't you like to know?"

"I asked, didn't I?"

"If you've got to ask, then you'll never know."

"Then I guess I'll never know because I stink at riddles and it seems that's all you speak in."

"Too bad," Maggie said, and made a move to leave.

"So, um," Josh said quickly, "I haven't seen you around here for a while."

"I've been working nights. It pays better. Why?"

"Well, I come to see Beck—"

Maggie brusquely interrupted. "Why?"

"She's a friend."

"Grown men don't make friends with six-year-old girls on dialysis, Mr. McCain."

"No? Well, maybe I'm not the man either of us thought I was."

Maggie's beeper sounded. She checked it. "I'm needed in pediatrics."

"Right. It was nice to see you again, Maggie."

"Yes, well " Uncomfortable, Maggie stuck out her hand.

Josh shook her hand, holding it an awkward second longer than either expected. Realizing that neither of them was going to say the words they both wanted to hear, Maggie turned and left.

19

FIRST-CLASS FOOLS

*R*osa sat in a booth going through the day's receipts with her calculator. She looked up and observed Josh in the next booth. He had his headphones on and was listening to an audiobook as he rubbed water-spots from the silverware and rolled it into napkins.

Rosa shook her head. "What is wrong with you?" she said accusingly.

"Cómo?" Josh said, removing his headphones.

"What is wrong with you?" Rosa repeated.

"Muchas cosas," Josh answered. "But I don't know which one you're talking about."

"A young man like you should have *una novia.*"

From the kitchen Alfonso said, "Ayy, Jozy. You have no respect for naked women."

"What?" Josh said, baffled.

"It's not healthy," Rosa continued. "Peoples need peoples, like Miss Streisand sings."

"No respect for naked…" Alfonso said.

"What's with the naked, Al? And it's Josh, not Jozy!"

"A lovely voice like that should know," Rosa said.

Alfonso chimed in again, "No respect for naked…"

86

Josh shook his head. "You guys are freaking me out."

The bells on the doorknob jingled, and in strutted an attractive woman in blue jeans and a low cut, flowery blouse. Her luxurious, curly black hair drew attention to her smooth shoulders and neckline. The pluck in her brown eyes gave them a ruby-like spark. For Josh, who had never seen Maggie dressed in anything but her bland white uniform, the look was transforming. Slack-jawed, he thought: *Wow, does she clean up well!*

"I'm sorry, dear," Rosa said. "We closed."

"I'm so sorry, but I'll just be a minute, okay?"

Not waiting for an answer, Maggie beelined it over to Josh's booth and slid into the seat opposite him. In order not to lose her nerve she got right to the point. "You really don't know anything about women, do you?"

"I'm discovering that there's quite a lot I don't know about, Maggie."

Josh looked over Maggie's shoulder and saw Rosa bouncing her eyebrows.

"Then you also probably don't know that there is a Marx Brothers film fest downtown at the Nickelodeon."

"Can you believe I've never seen a Marx Brothers film?"

"Honestly, no. But if that's true, then I see it as my civic duty to rectify your pathetic comic deficiency."

Maggie slid back out of the booth and stood tall. "Saturday, six o'clock in front of the theater. And don't keep me waiting. I loathe tardiness." She turned to Rosa, smiled, and shook Rosa's hand. "I apologize for my rudeness. I'm Maggie."

Rosa was all smiles. "Not at all, dear."

Maggie strode away leaving Josh blinking in bewilderment.

As soon as the door closed Rosa turned on Josh. "What is wrong with you? Why you not tell us you have pretty *novia*?"

"She's not my girlfriend."

From the kitchen came Alfonso's disappointed voice, "Ayy, Jozy, no respect—"

"Josh, Al—Josh!"

87

Rosa said, "You bring her to taste Daddy's fried ice cream!"

"Ayy, Jozy—"

Josh buried his face in his hands.

Outside, Maggie mumbled to herself as she hobbled to her car. She smacked her forehead in disbelief.

Don't worry, she thought, he won't show. And if he does, well, he'll be late, prove he's a jerk, and you can dump him before he gets any funny ideas. And if he's not the biggest jerk in the world...well, he'll break your heart just like the others. And then...oh! She threw her arms up in surrender. *How'd I ever become so neurotic?!*

Later that afternoon, Josh was still thinking about the day's unexpected event. He was equally confused. As he did his sit-ups on the grass, instead of counting, he sang and grunted the verses from Rod Stewart's classic song, "Maggie May."

"...Maggie ... I wish ... I'd never ... seen ... your face ... You made ... a first-class ... fool ... out of me ... But I'm ... as blind ... as a fool ... can be ... "

In rushed the same pooch that had been showing up for the past couple of months, only this time he brought two fellow mutts. The three dogs pounced on Josh and lapped at his face.

Laughing, Josh got up and started jogging. The dogs joined him, gamboling at his side.

20

RE-RIVALS

*T*he movie theater marquee read: *Marx Brother's Revival: Duck Soup, Horse Feathers, A Night At The Opera.*

Maggie stood impatiently in front of the box office. She checked her watch and shook her head. She wondered how she could feel both annoyed and relieved at the same time. When Josh leaped in front of her as she was about to leave, she knew instantly that it was relief that won the day. But heck if she was going to show it!

"You weren't leaving were you?" Josh said, out of breath. "I'm only five minutes late."

"Fifteen," Maggie said. "I was ten minutes early."

"Huh? Yeah, well, that's not *my* fault. Had I known—"

"Had you cared, you mean."

Josh grinned disarmingly. "What if I had been twenty minutes early making *you* ten minutes late? What then?"

Maggie folded her arms. "Honestly, Joshua McCain, have you ever been early for anything? Tell the truth."

"No... But—"

"All right. Just don't do it again."

She took Josh's arm. "Now come on, the popcorn is getting stale."

"You're insane, aren't you?" Josh said.

"No, just punctual."

Josh and Maggie shared a tub of popcorn and a single straw to a jumbo-sized cola. They both wondered if all that sharing meant anything, but pretended otherwise.

Groucho Marx said, "A child of five could understand this. Fetch me a child of five!"

Josh found this hilarious, and his laughter endeared him to Maggie. She was thrilled that he seemed to be enjoying something as corny and dated as a Marx Brothers film. She didn't think of the movies as passé herself, but as classics, and representative of an era when humor didn't have to be dark or vulgar. Maybe it made her appear old-fashioned, but for Maggie, caring what other people thought about her likes and dislikes was not among her insecurities.

As they exited the theater Josh entertained Maggie with his Groucho Marx impersonation. Maggie chuckled and gave him a playful shove.

"Watch," he said, "check me out. Like this, right…?" He stepped aside and broke into Groucho's trademark knee-spinning dance.

Maggie laughed and applauded. She sidled up to him. "I think you missed your calling."

Josh put his arm around Maggie's shoulder when suddenly they heard another set of clapping hands.

"Bravo," a female voice called out.

They turned and spotted Brooke Sievert clapping demurely. Josh's hand instantly recoiled from Maggie's shoulder—a fact that did not go unnoticed by either woman.

"What are you doing here?" Josh said coolly.

"This is the only theater I visit. Aren't you going to introduce me to your girlfriend?"

"This is my friend, Maggie. My Aunt Brooke. Maggie's a nurse."

"How do you do?" Maggie said.

"I take it you two met in the hospital," Brooke said.

"How did you—?"

"A barroom brawl, wasn't it?"

Maggie, arms folded, was finding their exchange very interesting.

"I know what you're thinking," Josh said. "Keep dreaming, Brooke. I'm right on schedule."

"Oh, Joshua," Brooke said, "we really should sit and talk. My idea on how we can both save a lot of time and money is still good. In fact, better. Fifty-fifty. After all, you and I are a lot alike, and so it's only natural we should split evenly."

"I'm nothing like you, Brooke."

"You clearly haven't my common sense, no," she agreed, and then glancing at Maggie, added, "or my tastes. But neither have you your father's willpower and spine. Let me help you. Otherwise, dear Joshua, you don't stand a chance."

"We'll see about that, Brooke. Come on, Maggie."

Josh took Maggie by the elbow and walked off with her. After a few steps he stuffed his hands safely into his pockets.

Turning the corner Maggie said, "What was that all about?"

"Nothing. A battle of wills, that's all." With newfound alacrity he said, "Come on. Rosa said she wants to treat you to a dish of Alfonso's amazing fried ice cream."

After making sure the coast was clear, he put his arm back around Maggie's shoulder.

Around the corner, Brooke snorted derisively and tapped at her cell phone.

"Mr. Tweene," she said snapped, "how hard can it be to force two-hundred grand down a dishwasher's throat? You see to it he stays away from that damn list, understand?"

21

SHAPE SHIFT

*J*osh jogged into his favorite corner of the park where he was greeted by his three training partners. "Mornin', Groucho!" he called. "Mornin', Chico! … Mornin', Harpo!"

The mutts answered with excited yaps and demanded a spirited tussle. Josh dropped to all fours and happily consented.

The dogs made it easier for Josh to get out in the morning because he knew they were expecting him. He thought of them as his personal trainers because of the way they followed him from spot to spot and barked at him like a drill sergeant. Josh didn't know why they took such a liking to him, but that they did made Josh feel somewhat distinguished.

The list required that he be able to do 150 consecutive push-ups, 30 pull-ups, and 200 sit-ups. He hadn't reached those marks yet, but he was closing in on them, and he knew that he could do it. The closer he got, the harder he tried. He even added additional exercises that weren't on the list: Hindu squats and push-ups, neck bridging, rope skipping, and lots of stretching.

Josh incorporated all this into his morning workout, and within a few short weeks he noticed a big improvement in his conditioning. Not only was he looking fitter, he had also become the most limber he had been since he was a rubbery toddler. This day he was even able to do the splits, something he once considered impossible for anyone but gymnasts and dancers. He was so excited that he yelled, "Groucho, Harpo, check me out! I'm doing the splits!" The dogs lifted up lazy eyelids, turned to one another unimpressed, and returned to their naps.

Because of his daily exercise, aikido workouts, Alfonso's cooking, and booze-free lifestyle, Josh felt he had attained a level of fitness he had never known before, and it felt good. Whenever he exercised, was on his bike, walking, or doing something monotonous like rolling silverware into napkins at Alfonso's, he continued to listen to his audiobooks. He also used the time to memorize and recite the twenty poems or passages that the list required. Already he had memorized poems by Ralph Waldo Emerson, Walt Whitman, Robert Frost, Emily Dickinson, William Ernest Henley's 'Invictus,' William Blake, Yeats, and Keats, as well as passages and psalms from the Bible.

Until now, Josh had spent his lifetime straight-arming and dodging anything resembling regimen or routine, especially one that included self-discipline. But now, through repetition and good, old-fashioned grit, he felt that he had smashed through some two-way mirror in his mind. On the other side of the mirror he discovered a different self, perhaps a higher self, one which had been waiting Josh's entire life to be recognized, and set free.

22

PARKED KARMA

*O*fficer Hank Miller bent down and noted the license plate number of a silver Mercedes parked beside an expired parking meter. His sizable stomach growled and he scribbled faster.

Behind him a voice called out, "I was just leaving!"

Officer Miller's stomach was in no mood to deal with another excuse before lunch. He didn't bother turning and continued writing his ticket. "Sorry, buddy. Tell it to the judge."

Mr. Tweene said, "I am the judge!"

"Huh?" Officer Miller turned and saw Mr. Tweene laughing and slapping his thigh. Officer Miller laughed along. "Aw, Bill, you son of a gun. How ya doin'?" They shook hands.

"Howdy, Hank, long time. You look good. Sylvia's been feeding you well, I see."

Hank patted his belly. "If only she'd do a little less baking and a little more shaking," he joked. "How's about you? I take it there is no shortage of jealous spouses out there to shadow?"

"It pays the bills."

Hank said, "You know I don't mind helping you out when I can. I can always use the spare change."

94

"Good, 'cuz I got a little favor to ask that'll keep you in beer and pretzels for a while."

"Husband or wife?" Hank asked.

"Nephew. The name is Joshua McCain. I need you to run a little background on him. The kid has way too much free time on his hands, and you know what they say about the devil finding work for idle hands, right?"

Hank nodded in comprehension. "Don't want the devil recruiting on my shift. Don't you worry."

~

At Alfonso's, lunch over, the dishes washed, and the silverware all rolled into napkins for the night shift, Josh sat at a table to finish Benjamin Franklin's *Autobiography and Other Writings*.

Rosa strolled up and stared at him like he was a Picasso painting. "*Qué haces* Mr. Einstein, every day with your books. You in school?"

"Nah. Been there, flunked that."

Through the window, Rosa saw Maggie strolling up, and waved to her. "Every day right on time. *Qué romántico.* You two kissing yet?"

"*Solamente amigos, Rosa.*"

Rosa shook her head, irked. "You read the wrong books, *muchacho.*"

Maggie swept into the restaurant and slid into the booth opposite Josh. "Hi, Rosa," she chirped.

"And you are *estúpida* for saying *nada,*" Rosa said, and huffed off.

Maggie tossed Josh a confused look. "I said hello."

From the kitchen Alfonso said, "Ayy, Muffie. No respect for kissing."

Maggie looked at Josh for an explanation. "Huh?"

Josh shrugged. "Don't worry, Muffie. You get used to it."

On the way back from Alfonso's, Josh stopped at the hardware store and bought some supplies for his apartment. The list required that Josh 'Make something old look new again,' and since he was tired of living in a hovel, he resolved he would spruce it up. He figured he would start by painting it, and so he picked up some plaster for the cracks, and chose an off-white paint to brighten up the place.

As he worked he listened to a Spanish language lesson on his cheap MP3 player. *"Hablo un poco de español,"* he repeated along. *"¿Favor de hablar más despacio? … ¿Favor de repitirlo?"*

Someone knocked at his door, but Josh couldn't hear it. Officer Hank Miller outside, however, could hear Josh.

"Hablo un poco de español … ¿Favor de hablar más despacio? … ¿Favor de repitirlo?"

The officer banged louder. Josh removed his headphones and opened the door.

"Joshua McCain?"

"No sé, depende. Por qué preguntas?"

"Wise guy, eh? *Comprende* this—?" The officer rifled through a stack of parking tickets with his thumb. He noted with pleasure Josh's stupefaction. "Eighteen-hundred dollars worth of overdue parking tickets, Señor McCain. Tell me, how do you say karma in Spanish?"

"Ay caramba!"

Officer Miller smirked. "That's what I thought."

"I don't have that kind of *dinero!*"

"Not my *problemo, amigo.* Tell it to the judge."

23

GEEZERLAND

*J*osh strolled into the Sunny Day Senior Center, and promptly slipped and fell onto the freshly mopped black and white tiled floor. Nobody noticed.

Old folk milled around, some on walkers, some in wheel-chairs, and most, he thought, in a daze. Volunteers lent helping hands. Despite its occupants, the center with its many windows and airy lobby wasn't as dreary as he imagined it would be.

Josh wandered through the lobby, swatting his thigh with a rolled-up sheet of paper, and grew steadily depressed. This was the last place he wanted to be. Why, he groused to himself, couldn't they have sent me to a nursery school or orphanage, or better yet, the Humane Society or some such place? But, *noooo*, they had to send me to *Geezerland*...

He stopped a woman pushing an old lady in a wheelchair. "Excuse me," he said. "I'm looking for Mrs. Johnson."

"Are you Josh?"

"Unfortunately, yeah."

Mrs. Johnson, a wafer-thin woman wearing big, rectangular eyeglasses with purple frames, fifty-four and perennially cheer-ful, shook his hand. "Welcome! It's nice to meet you. Call me

Sandy. Let me just cruise Mrs. Tucker here over to the TV room and I'll be right with you." She rolled the old woman away.

Josh scanned the premises where he was doomed to spend what he felt was eternity. He shook his head in despair, heaved a heavy sigh, and smacked the sheet of paper.

He strayed around the corner and observed the elderly of every make and color looking, for the most part, lost and lonely. Alongside a large garden window he spotted a dapper old fellow in a vintage suit sitting alone at a small table with a chessboard on it. The man stared at the board in senility.

Sandy Johnson returned, and they began a stroll through the center. "I understand you've volunteered for three days a week," she said cheerfully.

"I didn't exactly volunteer." Josh unrolled the paper, and handed it to Mrs. Johnson. The woman poked her glasses up on her small nose and studied the page. She arched an eyebrow. Josh added wanly, "I'll need your signature...regularly."

"I see," Sandy said. "May I ask what kind of trouble you got yourself into?"

"The judge said I'm parking-impaired."

"By the number of hours it seems your impairment is rather severe." Mrs. Johnson handed back the paper, a bright smile on her face. "Good," she chirped. "Most people quit after the first week. Looks like we've got you locked in. Have you any grand-parents, Josh?"

"No."

"Then cheer up, because now you've got about fifty. Follow me..."

Josh sighed and fell in behind her.

24

DISSED-APPOINTMENTS

*B*ecky sat frowning and forlorn in the waiting room with a copy of *Tom Sawyer* on her lap.

"I can read to you," her grandmother said.

"No," Becky mumbled. "I'll wait for Josh."

"You know, Becky, it's not good to place all your happiness in one person."

"Josh will come. He's my best friend."

"Remember, sweetie, Josh has a life too. He might be very busy and not able to visit you as often as he used to."

"Maybe he's mad at me. Maybe I said or did something and that's why he doesn't come anymore."

Speaking her thoughts made them more real, and she began to sniffle and cry. It wasn't a whining cry, but the cry of a breaking heart; one that burned the throat and stung the eyes, and drained the body of all joy.

Ms. Summers pulled Becky's head to her bosom and felt her quiver like a little bird. She stroked the girl's soft, brown hair and rocked her slowly.

"Josh is not mad at you, okay? He's just busy. I'm sure he'll visit you again when he can." *And when he shows his face, I'm going to give him a piece of my mind!*

~

Josh dashed into Alfonso's and met with Rosa's icy glare. She wiped at her brow with her sleeve and indicated the busy restaurant with a snubbing raise of her chin. It was the second time in three days that Josh had been late; the fifth time in two weeks; and each time he had been later than the last.

"Rosa, I'm sorr—"

Rosa was in no mood for his excuses, and shooed him off. Josh grabbed an apron and set to work clearing tables. He rushed into the kitchen and set down a tub of dirty dishes. Grabbing an empty bus tub and hurrying back out, he dropped a dish towel on the floor.

"Ayy, Jozy," Alfonso said, stirring a big pot. "If you drop something you must pick it up."

"In a minute, Al."

Alfonso shook his head in disappointed. "Ayy, Jozy. No respect for dropped things. No respect for time."

Josh stopped, sighed in resignation, and returned to pick up the towel.

"Josh," Rosa called out. "Hurry up in there! Customers are waiting!"

"I'm coming already," he said in frustration, and hustled back into the dining room.

~

On the Maggie front, things were no better since he began working at the Senior Center.

Weary from her night shift, Maggie dragged her feet into her apartment and dropped her purse and jacket onto the sofa. She checked her cell phone and saw a message from Josh.

She played the message and heard what she had come to expect: "Hey, Maggie. Sorry, but I gotta cancel on you again. I'm crazy busy these days. Call you soon, okay? Bye."

"A busboy's life is *very* stressful, isn't it Josh?" she muttered.

Maggie hit erase and ran a bath. When it was ready, she undressed and took off her prosthesis. She slipped into the warm sudsy water and glanced over the tops of the bubbles to the prosthesis lying on the floor beside the tub.

Although the accident that put her in the prosthesis was over ten years ago, whenever she was feeling lonely, as she was today, she couldn't look at the device without a heavy heart. The entire experience would come rushing back, only minus the physical pain.

From the distance of time she hovered over the despairing procedure. She recalled the amputated limb and waiting for the remaining stump to heal and shrink before it could be fitted with the prosthesis. Then, for several weeks, the stump was wrapped tightly with elastic bandages to help it shrink to a firm, smooth surface. During that time, she exercised the remaining limb muscles to promote circulation and preserve their strength and movement.

The next step in preparing the prosthesis involved making a plastic socket that would fit snugly over the stump. A cast for the socket was obtained by wrapping the stump with bandages soaked in wet plaster and then allowed to harden. The bandages formed a mold in which liquid plaster was poured to provide a model of the stump, and then a plastic socket was formed over the model. Finally, an artificial leg was attached to the socket. Maggie considered herself lucky that her knee had survived the accident and did not have to be replaced. The prosthesis ended in a substitute foot. No one but her doctor had ever seen her stump.

Although susceptible to melancholy from time to time, Maggie had moved well beyond the stage of self-pity. She often went weeks thinking little of her condition. At times she was almost grateful for her misfortune, for she knew it changed her in fundamental ways that she would not want to exchange in return for her leg, if she could: a fantasy that she occasionally succumbed to, but never with good consequence.

The accident and an ensuing friendship with a nurse put her on the road to nursing; a job that she loved, and from which she knew tremendous satisfaction. Her trials taught her self-discipline, courage, and above all, that she was more than her body; a body, in fact, that her girlfriends had envied, that had won her athletic trophies in high school, and dates with college men.

No, she would not turn back the clock if it meant forgetting and losing all the other triumphs and wisdom she had gained. Still, did it mean she had to be lonely forever? Would there never be someone with whom she could share her strength, her dreams, and her love?

And that brought her back to Josh the busboy whom she couldn't even count on to show up on time for a cup of coffee. Maggie grabbed up a handful of bubbles and blew them away. Faith, she told herself. There will be others.

Kazu glanced at the English study materials in the corner of the *dojo*. He turned questioningly to Curtis, his senior student. Curtis peered outside, and shrugged. Kazu frowned and redirected his attention to his aikido students. It was the third class in a row that Josh had either missed or been rudely late for, both aikido and English.

Although Kazu knew that only a small percentage of students had what it took to continue for long with the rigors of learning a martial art, he had had high hopes for Josh.

He was angry with Josh, not so much for failing him, but for proving him mistaken. Kazu considered himself a good judge of character, and Josh apparently did not have what Kazu thought he did. Aikido, Kazu believed, had taught him to see into the essence of a person. Perhaps, he ruminated, his aikido was lacking. Maybe he should close the *dojo*. *If I am mistaken in the judgment of my students and friends, I am not worthy of instructing them in the way of ki…*

He would discuss it with his wife, Keiko, he thought. She was the only person who could see into his own heart. Keiko would know, and she would tell him if she thought he had lost his touch.

Kazu glanced again at the English materials. He had been studying hard on his own, and was happy with his progress. He enjoyed his classes with Josh, and thought Josh was a natural teacher. Don't give up on him yet, he thought. In the meantime, you must not let your concern interfere with your own students.

The *sensei* gave his *hakama* a determined tug. He thought he hadn't scolded his students recently. He put on a grim face and made an example of a couple of youths, putting the fear of God in the others. He made sure that by the time the class was finished, their uniforms were soaked with sweat.

Knitting needles in hand, and no idea how to begin, Josh sat at his card table and stared dismally at a dozen balls of yarn. Out of boredom and frustration, he changed his grip and held the needles like chopsticks. He tried picking up one of the balls like it was *sushi*. He fumbled it, and numbly watched as the ball of yarn rolled off the table, and unwound across the floor.

Finally, he got up to see what else he could start on from the list. He ran his finger down the items and tapped on: *Cook a seven-course meal*. He grabbed his wallet and went to the grocery store.

Two hours later, a cookbook in his hand, flour on his face, and sweat on his brow, Josh struggled in his tiny, messy kitchen. A timer went off, a pot boiled over, and in a hurry to prevent disaster, he cut and then burned his finger.

"Ow! Shi—!" He flung the cookbook at the wall.

After calming himself he returned to the list and decided to work on the item: *Learn five magic tricks.*

Band-Aids on his fingers, he consulted a book on magic tricks that he had checked out of the library. He practiced a card trick, trying to make a card disappear and reappear with the flick of his hand, but his fingers would not cooperate. He gave them a vigorous shake and tried some more. It was to no avail, and he fumbled or flung one card after another.

Beside himself with frustration, he lashed out and accidentally smacked his recently burned fingers against the nearby counter top. "Ow! God…! Shi—!"

Readying himself for bed, Josh pondered the list. He spent the entire day trying to make sense of it, trying to make a dent in it, but all had ended in failure.

Nothing was going right. Alfonso and Rosa were mad at him; Kazu probably hated him by now; Becky must have been wondering why he hadn't been in to see her for over two weeks; and Ms. Summers was likely thinking, 'I told you so.' Then there was Maggie. The last time he spoke to her he could tell by her voice that she was upset with him. She didn't deserve this, he thought. None of these people deserved this.

Josh sighed. "Who am I kidding?"

He switched off the light and crossed the room in the dark towards his bed. On the way he stepped on a knitting needle. He yelped, and holding his foot and hopping on one leg, he cried, "Shit, shit, *shit!*"

25

LA CUCARACHA

*J*osh limped down a back street in the industrial side of town, his foot smarting from the previous evening's impalement. He recognized the old warehouse and entered.

In contrast to its outside, inside the warehouse was tidy and stylish: a showroom for Chad Jefferson's wood and metal artwork. Behind the wall that separated the factory from the showroom, Josh heard the sound of welding. He wandered behind the wall and stood silently observing Chad as he welded away on a metal sculpture that he had been commissioned to make for the lobby of a new hotel.

Chad looked up, turned off his torch and lifted his goggles. "You're wasting precious time, Josh."

"Yours?"

"No. Yours."

"I can't do it, Chad."

"Fine. Call Jeffrey and collect your booby prize."

"The list is too long. Half the things I know nothing about and haven't a clue where to begin. Cooking, knitting—" Josh held up his hands showing Chad his Band-Aids. "This is what I know about cooking."

Chad whipped off his gloves and rolled up his sleeves revealing a number of nasty-looking welts and scars. "This is what I once knew about welding and woodworking," Chad replied, peeved. "If you're looking for sympathy you won't find it here."

"I'm not look—. If Dad wanted me out of his will, why didn't he just say so? This list, Chad, it's like…" Josh fought back his tears. "It's like he hated my guts or something."

Chad fixed Josh with an indignant squint. "He loved you more than you'll ever know."

"I rated, all right," Josh said. "He took a knife in the gut saving a sixteen-year-old crackhead from getting the crap beat out of him in a New York subway, and for me he left a roll of potty-paper-long punishments because I failed him as a son. Chad, that kid was so strung out he couldn't even remember what Dad did for him! What am I supposed to think?"

Chad turned solemn. "He was dying, Josh."

"I wish he had died, then Dad would still be here!"

"Cancer. The doctors gave him six months."

"What?" Josh said, incredulous. "*Dad?* No, no, he never…"

"What difference would it have made? Honestly, Josh, what would you have done differently, huh?"

Josh stammered, "I-I just don't get him, Chad."

"Listen," Chad said, "I'm not gonna stand here and tell you what kind of a man your dad was. You want to know who he was? You want inside his head? The answer is in that list some-where. It's hard, yeah, but not impossible. *Not* impossible." Chad pulled down his goggles and went back to work.

Josh stood speechless. His thoughts spun like a slipped bicycle chain unable to catch on any gear. Finally, he turned to leave.

"Yo…" Chad called. Josh turned and caught a hardbound notebook. "Your dad's last journal. He said to give it to you if you stopped by. It won't tell you who he was, but it'll tell you who he wasn't." Chad returned to his work.

Lost in thought, Josh cycled lethargically through the neighborhoods he had come to know. He gravitated to the park. There he sat on a bench and read his father's journal. When the sun set behind the trees, Josh read the final page. He closed the journal. His face quivered and fell into his hands. "I need you, Dad," he croaked, and then he broke into sobbing, shoulder-heaving grief.

Having exhausted himself, Josh wiped his tears with his shirt sleeves and remounted his bike. He rode aimlessly for three hours, absorbed in memories of his father, and racked with guilt and regrets that he knew he could never erase. At last he headed towards home and peddled past Alfonso's restaurant. Through the restaurant's glass door, Josh saw the silhouette of a man sitting alone in the dark. Josh dismounted for a better look. He saw Alfonso in his chef's uniform sitting on a chair, gazing distantly at the floor. That it was late and Alfonso was still in uniform suggested that he had been there for some time.

Josh tested the door and found it unlocked. He entered without a word. Alfonso ignored him. One of the booths had been pulled away from the wall and Alfonso was staring at the floor behind it in a state of deep contemplation.

Josh pulled up a chair beside Alfonso and sat with him. For an hour they stared at the wall together in complete silence. Alfonso took a sudden interest in something. He rose and tiptoed toward the wall. Stealthily, he removed a rolled-up newspaper from his coat pocket. He squatted onto his haunches and —*whack!*—he killed a cockroach.

Alfonso turned to Josh and nodded profoundly. "Ayy, Jozy, we have more patience than *una cucaracha. Eso es bueno.*" He addressed the dead bug. "Señor Cucaracha, you had no respect for clean floors."

After disposing with the cockroach, Alfonso walked over to Josh and set his chef's hat on the young man's head. His arm around Josh's shoulders, he walked him into the kitchen and to the back pantry. He pointed to a three-ringed notebook on a top shelf. Josh kicked over a footstool and grabbed it. He noted the yellowed strip of paper taped to the cover. In large, handwritten scrawl was written: *Alfonso's Recipes*.

Josh handed the book to Alfonso and they walked back into the kitchen. Alfonso set it down next to the gas range and turned to Josh. "We begin with the most basic of food, *frijoles*. A great philosopher once said that beans were *malo*. He was an idiot. Beans are *bueno*! And Alfonso's beans are *muy, muy bueno*."

Josh chuckled, put his arm around Alfonso's waist and observed and listened as the master chef, in his inimitable way, demonstrated that Pythagoras's theory of beans was full of gas.

Ready for bed, Josh pondered the list on the wall. Having forgotten to tear away yesterday's page from the *Butt-buster Calendar*, he revealed a quote from the German poet, Wolfgang Goethe:

Friday, June 2

"Whatever you can do, or dream you can, begin it. Boldness has genius, power, and magic in it."
— Wolfgang Goethe (1749–1832), German poet, novelist, philosopher, and scientist.

Hold on, didn't—?

Josh strode into the other room and picked up his father's journal. He flipped through it and came to the same quotation, written in his father's own scrawl. Josh grinned and looked up to heaven, "You talking to me?"

Only his father had gone one step further than the *Butt-buster Calendar*. Taylor McCain had followed the quotation with another quote that he said was mistakenly attributed to Goethe, but actually belonged to William H. Murray from his book, *The Scottish Himalayan Expedition*.

Josh reread it. This time the quote took on a significance that eluded him in the park on account of his grief and self-pity. Now the words felt as if they were directed specifically at Josh himself.

"Until one is committed, there is hesitancy, the chance to draw back, always ineffectiveness. The moment one definitely commits oneself, then Providence moves too. A whole stream of events issues from the decision, raising in one's favor all manner of unforeseen incidents and meetings and material assistance, which no man could have dreamed would have come his way."

Josh hit the light and crossed the room to his bed. He lay down and stared at the ceiling in contemplation.

Had 'Providence' been at work in his life? He thought about his chance meetings with Kazu. He thought of Alfonso and Rosa, and of Becky and Maggie. Was it only coincidence that the bolder and more determined his actions and efforts, the more they coincided with persons that assisted him in his work? If so, how would that explain the Senior Center setback and all the trouble that had cost him? Josh reached for the alarm clock on the bedside stand. He turned the alarm hand from 8:30 a.m. to 5:00 a.m. There was only one way to find out.

26

BABY STEPS

*B*zzz…
      Josh smacked the alarm and whimpered. A curious radiance emanating from outside his window grabbed enough of his attention to keep his drooping eyelids from slamming shut. He sat up, and with a swipe of his hand, flung open the curtains. Dawn's rosy fingers were spreading out over the city. *So, that's what you look like.* He had gone to bed at dawn many times in his life, but typically too drunk to notice or care. Today was the first time he could remember that he and Aurora, the goddess of dawn, had risen together.

Josh rolled out of his covers and slouched to the bathroom. He tore away Goethe's aphorism and put it aside to later tape to the wall among his other favorites. He read the new quote and appreciated the timing:

Saturday, June 10
"Morning is when I awake and there is a dawn in me."
— Henry David Thoreau, *Walden*

Off he jogged. Everything about his neighborhood was

different at this hour—fresher, more tranquil, even friendlier. A paperboy and various delivery men waved to him in early morning camaraderie, as did a group of Orthodox Jews, or maybe Hasidim—he didn't know—on an early morning stroll. The older ones had beards, and they wore skullcaps or brimmed hats, and dark nineteenth-century garb. Josh waved to everyone he met; and everyone waved back. He felt as if he had become a member of an elite club of early risers.

He ran on.

The bakery delivery man hollered, "Yo!" Josh turned and saw a bagel arching through the air towards him. He snagged it, shouted thanks, and continued on his way, munching as he went. What a difference a few hours made, he thought. Right next door, separated only by a few winks of sleep was a whole new world.

Josh finished his morning exercises that day at the high school football field. It was time to see how far along he had progressed. He hadn't tried sprinting a full mile since the day he puked in the long jump pit. Huffing, his lungs on fire, Josh sprinted across the finish line and clicked his stopwatch. He bent over in exhaustion to catch his breath, and checked the time. He couldn't believe his eyes: 5:45. He shook his head and walked off the run. *Forty-five seconds!* It might as well have been forty-five minutes, he thought dismally.

Alfonso's restaurant was closed on weekends, so after a shower and a bowl of cornflakes, Josh read, studied Spanish, and worked on his apartment. He was amazed at how much he could accomplish by noon, which found him over at the Sunny Day Senior Center sitting in the lunchroom spoon-feeding ninety-five-year-old Mrs. Walker.

Mrs. Walker gummed her food and Josh swiped at her mouth with the regularity of a windshield wiper. Beside him stood a mountain of used napkins. When Josh began working at the Sunny Day Senior Center, many of his duties grossed him out; now he took them in stride. Had he just become inured to the drudgery? Or did he matriculate to a higher level of maturity? He didn't know. But one thing was certain: he learned a new respect for Maggie, who did harder and ickier work every day, and never complained to him about any of it either.

He missed Maggie. He had seen her only a couple of times in the past month, and a chill had settled between them. He blamed himself. He considered explaining his aloofness by confiding in her about the list, his situation, and what he was trying to do. Maybe she'd understand.

Then again, if he succeeded in completing the list, he would be fabulously rich, and he feared that even someone as principled as Maggie might see him differently with such knowledge. Besides, he had to stay focused. Although he had made much progress, he knew he still had a long way to go, and a romantic relationship would only distract him; especially one where physical intimacy was forbidden. To paraphrase a quip from Oscar Wilde and the *Butt-buster Calendar*, Josh felt he "could resist anything but temptation."

No, he would tell no one. Kyle, of course, knew about the list, but Josh figured that Kyle had probably forgotten about it. They hadn't spoken since their last meeting in the hospital, and even if Kyle did think about Josh or the list, Josh felt sure that his friend, understandably, didn't think he had a snowball's chance in hell of ever completing it.

Still, Josh missed his wry friend, and often thought of calling him to see how he was doing, but he was too ashamed to do so. Surely, Kyle would ask him what he was up to, and how would he answer? *'Oh, washing dishes and waiting on tables at a Mexican restaurant. Working off a couple grand in parking tickets at an old folks' home. Sort of dating a one-legged girl I haven't even kissed. Reading Epictetus and going to bed at ten…'*

His thoughts returned to the list. He still needed to find ways to accomplish some of the odder demands that the list entailed. But where could he possibly learn such things? Who did he know with such expertise? Moreover, even if he did find such instructors, he couldn't pay them. He was barely eking by as it was. And even though he was determined to get a head start on every day, where could he fit it all in? They were discouraging thoughts, and he fought them back the best he could.

Josh looked up and took notice of the old man sitting alone at the chessboard by the window. There he was every day, a permanent fixture, always dressed neatly in a vintage suit, staring blankly at the chessboard, oblivious to all around him. Josh wondered what kept the old geezer ticking. What or who was he waiting for? The Grim Reaper? No one at the home could recall hearing the old man speak since he was admitted some five years earlier. Not a word.

The sound of a blues harmonica drifted into the lunchroom snapping Josh from his reverie. He noticed that Mrs. Walker's head began to bob to the music.

"You like that, eh, Mrs. Walker?"

The old lady continued to gum her food and stare at some memory in her mind.

Josh stopped a passing volunteer. "Jane, would you mind taking over here a minute. I'll be right back." Jane nodded and Josh grabbed a full napkin holder from another table and set it down in front of her. "You're gonna need these."

Josh followed the music through the center. He slowed as he passed the elderly gent seated at the chessboard, but decided to keep going. He turned a corner and saw a gray-haired black man sitting alone on a folding chair in a small side room playing the harmonica. The man acknowledged Josh with smiling eyes, but kept on playing. Josh looked on and listened.

Josh promised himself that he would not let the day go without paying Kazu a visit. He had been avoiding him out of shame. It was time to face him, but how, he wondered, could he show Kazu how sorry he was, and that things would be different from now on? He knew that Kazu was not impressed by words, and "sorry" would probably only insult the man. He showed up at the *dojo* in his *gi* and said nothing.

Josh didn't have to say or do anything. Kazu did Josh's apologizing for him, meting out Josh's punishment the old-fashioned way. Josh was to be the day's tackling dummy, and practice was to be one that neither Josh nor any other of the students should forget. Every student took turns slamming Josh to the *tatami* as they practiced their techniques. *Bam!* ... *Bam!* ... down he went, over and over. Kazu observed Josh's drubbing stern-faced and ominously silent.

Josh stoically took the beating. He felt he had it coming. He didn't know if doing so would be enough to earn back Kazu's respect, but neither was he going to give Kazu the pleasure of forcing him to complain, cry, or quit.

After thirty minutes of pounding, Kazu decided that he wanted to demonstrate a new move. He called on Josh to attack him. Josh charged. Kazu slammed Josh to the *tatami* like he was a rag doll.

"Again!" Kazu ordered. Josh staggered to his feet and rushed at him again. Kazu expertly slung him smashing into the floor. Josh groaned and slapped the *tatami* in frustration.

Kazu said, "Like baby, you falls many time before walk."

Josh wobbled to his feet and looked Kazu defiantly in the eyes. "No, Sensei," he said. Slowly and distinctly, Josh corrected him: "Like a baby, you must fall many times before you can walk."

Kazu's eyes narrowed, and then a sliver of a grin cracked his austere and stony face.

"Repeat!" Josh commanded.

Kazu said, "Like a baby, you must fall many times before you can walk."

"Yes!" Josh said jubilantly.

"Now *you* repeat!"

Josh charged Kazu and the sensei slammed him mercilessly to the mat. Josh moaned and his classmates hooted with laughter.

27

SILENCE IS GOLDEN

When Josh first showed his face again at the hospital after his extended absence, Becky wouldn't even acknowledge his presence by sticking out her tongue. Instead, she sniffed and pretended to ignore him by talking to the rag doll her grandmother had recently bought for her.

Josh frowned and squatted on his haunches in front of Becky. "I see you have a new friend."

"Oh," Becky said to the doll, "don't mind him. He's not a good friend."

"Becky's right, little missy," Josh said to the doll. "I haven't been a very good friend. I've been so bad that Becky won't talk to me anymore. Do you think you could tell her that I'm very sorry, and that I promise to be a good friend from now on?"

"What?" Becky said, putting the doll's face to her ear. "Oh, really? Humph, I don't think he means it. Tell him I'm not interested." She turned the doll to Josh who pretended to listen, nodding along and frowning.

"I see ... Uh-huh ... Really? That's too bad because—" Josh leaned in close to the doll and pretended to whisper in its ear.

Becky pulled the doll away and said, "What did he say?" She

put the doll's face to her ear again. "Well, I suppose it's *possible*. But he should know that two strikes and you're out! But I'll have to ask my grammy first." Becky turned to Ms. Summers. "Daisy said that Josh wants to take me for a pony ride this weekend. Can I go?"

"Huh?" Josh said.

"A pony ride?" Ms. Summers said, smirking mischievously. "I didn't know there was a place to ride ponies near here. But sure, honey, as long as he promises not to forget. Like you say, two strikes and you're out."

Josh gulped. *Uh-oh...*

Josh figured that making peace with Maggie would prove even harder than it was to track down the only pony within a bus ride of town. If only Maggie could be appeased by a pony ride, he thought.

But no, he knew Maggie would insist on *talking*. And it was 'talking' that had always doomed him in the past. It was only a year ago that his talk with Julie ended up with her pelting him with pasta and stuffing a rubber tree plant into his arms. When he dropped by Maggie's apartment he made sure he wasn't wearing anything that he wouldn't mind having to throw away.

Maggie was surprised to see him, but she invited him in and kindly offered him a cup of ginger tea. Josh said thank you, but he was worried about there being scalding liquids anywhere near their upcoming conversation. Maggie kept quiet as she prepared the tea, and her silence made Josh squirm. He had never tasted ginger tea. It was lightly sweetened and very good.

He had to hand it to Maggie. She surprised him. She didn't cry. She didn't raise her voice. She didn't throw anything at him. Her talking was all one-way, and he liked that. She was a lecturer, and he'd been receiving lectures his entire life. All he had to do was nod and look repentant. Besides, her sermon wasn't half bad. He thought it ranked up there with some of the best ones his dad delivered to him when he was younger.

Maggie didn't resort to name-calling or even call into question his manhood. She didn't get testy, and she didn't demand an apology. She was philosophical. She wanted him to understand a few things. She appealed to his reason, to his emotions, and to his higher self. She put words in his mouth and thoughts in his head.

He didn't dare interrupt her. She was on a roll.

Besides, everything he thought of saying he knew would have only sounded juvenile, and juvenile was the *last* thing he needed to come across as now. Maggie remained composed, even regal throughout her speech.

She spoke about honesty, sincerity, and consideration, and she threw in some elucidating examples that she had observed from her loving parents and a couple she knew back in England: Cecilia and Timothy, who, apparently, had developed openness and trust to an art form. Maggie spoke about the significance of integrity and friendship, the meaning of loyalty and camaraderie, and what a woman wants. This last part shocked him, for every man he ever knew swore there was no knowing the secret of what a woman wants. According to Maggie, however, it was quite simple, and it only took as long as brewing and drinking two more pots of tea to divulge it.

By the end, about two hours later, Josh nearly bolted to his feet with applause. Man, that was good, he thought. You *rock*, Maggie! He wondered how big a part her British accent played in her lofty and inspired sermon. But he said nothing, because nothing seemed to be working really well for him. He was afraid that anything he might say would be misinterpreted, and so saying nothing at all was the safest bet.

After three pots of tea Josh really, *really* had to pee; so badly, that he had begun to perspire. Still, even with that pain and discomfort, he didn't dare ask to use her bathroom. He was terrified that even excusing himself to use the toilet might be misconstrued, and so blow his chance for an altercation-free evening.

Josh stood, put on his most contrite face—which came easily because his bladder felt like it was about to explode—and said, "Thank you, Maggie."

"Okay, then," Maggie said. "Pick me up tomorrow at eight for ice cream."

Josh smiled. "It's a date." He turned, walked out the door, waddled down two flights of stairs holding his crotch, and relieved himself for two long, glorious minutes behind an elm tree. He rode home on his bike at peace with the world and everyone in it.

Upstairs, Maggie leaned against the door shaking her head. She thought: Oh, you've really blown it this time. You're such a bully! The poor guy was almost in tears at the end. And that stuff about Cecilia and Timothy, where in the world did you come up with those names? He had to see right through it. Men aren't *that* stupid. Mom and Dad? *Puh-lease!* Their rows were notorious. And what was that I was going on about women wanting? Yeah, right, maybe the *sane* women in the world!

Maggie sighed and began getting ready for bed, but she couldn't put the evening out of her head. He won't come tomorrow, she concluded, and I can't blame him. I eviscerated the poor guy. There were beads of sweat on his forehead! She changed into her pajamas, but she wasn't tired and knew it was going to be a long, worry-wracked night.

28

PROVIDENCE PURLING

*J*osh threw on his sweats and bounded out onto the street. He jogged off towards the park. On the way he saw Bagel Guy right on schedule making his early morning rounds. Josh jogged towards him.

"What'll it be today, Josh?" Bagel Guy called out.

"Raisin!"

Josh jogged up, handed off a quarter, and kept running. "Going long!" he hollered. Bagel Guy reared back his arm and flung the bagel arching through the air. Josh snagged the roll, took a bite, waved, and kept running.

After study and a shower, Josh rinsed his razor and banged it against the side of the bathroom sink. He grabbed a towel, turned to his *Butt-buster Calendar*, and ripped away Saturday's page.

Sunday, August 13
"Correct thy son, and he shall give thee rest; yea, he shall give delight unto thy soul."
— Proverbs 29:17

He ran his finger down the list taped beside the mirror and stopped at the task: *Regularly attend a religious service of your choice.*

Josh wiped the remaining shaving cream from his face and walked to the closet. He pulled out the one hanger still draped in dry-cleaning plastic and ripped open the bag. It was the only suit he hadn't pawned. To his surprise, he had to cinch his belt three holes over just to keep his pants up.

The last time Josh had been to church was with his mother for Christmas mass almost twenty years earlier. She died one month later. His father asked him many times over the years to go to church with him, "as a favor to me," he'd say, but each time Josh had "something important to do."

Now, sitting in the pew listening to Father Tillack guide his flock through the service, Josh couldn't recall a single one of those somethings that had taken precedence over going to church with his father. He pictured his dad sitting by himself in that same church every Sunday, head bowed, praying for him, as Josh knew he surely did. His eyes misty with remorse, Josh felt a wretched loneliness, for his father and himself.

Until now Father Tillack hadn't noticed Josh, but when he looked up from his Bible and requested his congregation to join him in a hymn, their eyes met. Father Tillack smiled as he sang, and Josh smiled back, the hymn hovering on his lips.

Josh spent the rest of the day at the library. He found a vacant computer and typed 'McCain Industries' into the search engine. The engine retrieved hundreds of links. He clicked one and pulled out a pen and legal pad. He began taking notes.

Later, he sat at a library table with a stack of old magazines and newspapers. Before him was a newspaper with the headline: *McCain Industries Heads List of New Jersey's Fastest Growing Companies.* In the social calendar of another old paper he took interest in an article entitled: *Self-made McCain to Marry Socialite*

Victoria Price. Of equal interest was a feature article on his dad in a fifteen-year-old edition of Fortune magazine entitled: *Taylor McCain Means Business.* By the time the library closed, Josh had filled up two yellow legal pads with notes.

When Josh returned home, he picked up where he had left off sanding the worn wooden floor. As he sanded and applied a coat of lacquer he repeated along with his Spanish tape. *"De quién es este lápiz? Ese lápiz es mío…"*

He spent the evening sitting at his table practicing making a playing card disappear and reappear with the flick of his hand. One after another the cards shot away from his fingers landing among a pile of failures.

It was tough throwing off sleep the following morning, and Josh even nodded off again in his chair as he tied his shoes. After nearly slipping to the floor, he shook himself alert and dragged himself out the door.

Once outside in the crisp morning air he came to his senses. He snagged another bagel from Bagel Guy and shared it with his personal trainers: Groucho, Harpo, and Chico, who were waiting for him in the park, tails wagging, and eager to bark their orders. Somehow their uncanny canine senses had figured out that he had moved up his timetable. Josh chuckled thinking they were as punctual as Maggie.

Sometimes, like today, the dogs encouraged him by more than just their ever-cheerful company. As Josh did his pull-ups, he suddenly felt Chico, the smallest of the three mutts, latch onto his pant leg. The extra weight made Josh strain all the more to get his head over the bar. He tried to shake the pooch loose, but the little fellow was a determined coach. The other dogs, heads cocked, looked on. Josh managed two more pull-ups and then busted out laughing. He dropped to the ground, whereupon the pooches pounced and smothered him with doggie kisses and snuggles.

Once a week Josh went to the high school track and attempted to break the necessary five-minute mile. Again, gulping for air, he clicked the stopwatch as he crossed the finish line. He checked the watch: 5:35. Josh shook his head in deep disappointment, and walked off the run. Thirty-five seconds may as well have been thirty-five miles, he thought.

~

The veracity of the lines his father had quoted from William H. Murray did not escape Josh's consciousness when he began finding tutors, coaches, and trainers all around him:

> *"...the moment one definitely commits oneself, then Providence moves too. A whole stream of events issues from the decision, raising in one's favor all manner of unforeseen incidents and meetings and material assistance, which no man could have dreamed would have come his way."*

Indeed, The Sunny Day Senior Center was proving to be not only a blessing in disguise, but also a veritable university. Not all the elderly were senile or incapacitated, and Josh came to discover that some of them were more than happy to share some one or another talent with him. None of them knew or cared to know why Josh wanted their help; they were just happy to feel needed. Josh often stayed beyond his required time if he didn't have other responsibilities, and even began stopping by the Center on the days he wasn't scheduled to work. Today was one such day.

An affable, prune-faced woman in a wheelchair, Mrs. Applebee had become Josh's knitting teacher. He told Mrs. Applebee that he wanted to knit a sweater. She began by teaching him the two basic stitches of knit and purl. She told him that after he got a hang of those, she would add other stitches like the rib stitch for the bottom, cuffs, and neckline of the sweater. To make the sweater more decorative she would then teach him the cable stitch.

Most knitters, Mrs. Applebee informed him, follow written patterns that contain a standard vocabulary of abbreviations. She said he had to learn those, and gave it to him as "homework." A pattern, she told him, gives directions on the types of stitches used, the order in which they are used, and the size and shape of the finished piece of fabric. Knitting was a lot more complicated than he imagined, and thanks to Mrs. Applebee's good-natured patience and wry humor, more fun, too. Once past his initial fear and frustration, he found it meditative and a good way to end each evening.

Mrs. Applebee checked Josh's work, shook her head, and pointed at his mistakes. Josh's ears perked up. Blues Man was up from his afternoon nap, and his harmonica was once again charging the air with its toe-tapping rhythm.

"Hold that thought, Mrs. Applebee, okay? I'll be back in a bit."

"Okay," she said, "but at my age, thoughts tend to lose their way."

"And at my age," Josh replied, "I wouldn't know the difference anyway." He pecked her on the cheek and scooted off, following the music. He passed the spruced old man sitting alone by the garden window gazing as usual at the chessboard in a state of senility. The old man took no notice of Josh as he breezed by.

Josh entered Blues Man's room. The door was always open. The room was small and simple with powder blue walls. The centerpiece was a dresser with a mirror, and stuck into the border of the mirror were a dozen old snapshots of Blues Man and his band.

The old timer looked up and nodded in welcome. Josh nodded back, reached into his pocket, and pulled out a harmonica. Blues Man chuckled. He pulled a folding chair up beside him and gave it a pat. Josh sat down and Blues Man began to teach him how to hold the instrument.

Later, on his way back to the main lobby, Josh strolled past the senile old man by the window again. He noticed that the guy hadn't moved a muscle in almost an hour. Josh halted, backpedaled, and slipped into the chair opposite him, the chess board between them. The man didn't bat an eye.

For a long minute Josh sat quietly sizing up the situation. Then, as if in a dare, Josh pushed forward a pawn. He waited. The old man showed no response. Josh waited some more. If the codger could dress himself and find his way to the same place every day, something in him was still alive, Josh thought. The old man lifted his arm, and with deliberateness he moved his pawn. Wordlessly they began to play. In one-minute flat Josh was checkmated.

"You suck," the old man snorted.

"I know. I'm Josh."

The man looked up. "Berkowitz."

"Nice to meet you, Berkowitz."

"Play again?" Berkowitz grumbled.

29

YEAR TWO

"*The highest reward for man's toil is not what he gets for it but what he becomes by it.*"
— *John Ruskin (1819-1900)*

30

A FISHER OF MEN

*M*r. Hillman looked up and furled his brow in annoyance.

"Don't worry," Josh said, "I'm not here for money."

"Then what do you want? I'm busy." He gestured to the crowded bank lobby and the lines of people.

"Lunch."

"You want me to buy you lunch?" Mr. Hillman said, incredulous.

Josh smiled. "No. I want to buy you lunch."

"I'm not hungry. Now if you'd kindly—"

"And in exchange, I'm hoping you might share with me some of those stories you said you have about my father. Do you like Mexican food, Mr. Hillman?"

∼

Josh and Mr. Hillman arrived at Alfonso's after the lunch rush. Josh informed Mr. Hillman that this was where he worked now, and that if he didn't mind, he would like to order for him. Bob Hillman nodded and admitted he didn't really know a *tamale* from a *tostada*.

Rosa and Alfonso came out to meet Mr. Hillman, and Josh introduced them to him. Rosa poured on the sweetness, which Josh found comical. Hillman was just a banker, after all, but she treated him like he was royalty. Josh guessed it was his suit and tie that impressed her. Most of her clientele dressed in jeans and T-shirts. Alfonso did some ingratiating too, which took the form of a few self-promoting stories.

Hillman found the couple amusing and the experience novel. He detected in the pair a real fondness for Josh, and that intrigued him. Seeing the way the elderly Alfonso responded to "Jozy," and enjoyed being in his company endeared the lad to Bob Hillman somewhat. He never really disliked Josh; he just thought him an ungrateful slacker. When Josh had worked for him he knew Josh to be quite popular with the other employees, especially the women. But his job wasn't to be popular; it was to get work done, and Josh was insufferably irresponsible and incompetent. The only reason he kept him on as long as he did was out of respect for Taylor McCain.

Hillman had to admit that there was something different about the boy since he had last seen him. For one, he was courteous; never an adjective he thought he'd ever use to describe Joshua McCain. The boy seemed more at peace with himself, and fitter too. He wondered what might have been behind his transformation. Sure, a lot can happen in a year, but he had known many Joshuas in his lifetime, and none had ever grown up to be anything other than fleshier, balder, and more pathetic copies of the younger man.

"You were right," Hillman said, dabbing his mouth with a napkin. "Those were the best beans I've ever tasted."

Josh smiled, proud of Alfonso and his beans.

"So you want to know how your dad changed my life, huh?"

"If you don't mind."

"More than one way," Hillman said. "For starters, I ran into some legal problems some years back. No need to rehash it, but I was being sued for a lot of money for something I didn't do.

The fellow suing me was a lawyer and a damn good one. I didn't think I stood a chance. I didn't have money for good legal advice and I thought I was doomed. Your dad introduced me to his friend—"

"Jeffrey Barnes," Josh said with a knowing chuckle.

Hillman laughed. "Ah, so you know where this is going?"

"Barnes ripped the guy a new one."

"Damn right he did. That hotshot was putty in Barnes' hands. It was beautiful. Not only did I win, Barnes sued the guy right back and I got a good chunk of change. Ever since, Mr. Barnes has represented me, and the bank too. He's been a godsend."

"That's great, what else?"

"Your dad introduced me to my wife, Laura."

"Really? I didn't even know you were married."

"Eight years next month. She's the best thing that ever happened to me, and if you met her, you'd wonder how the heck a balding bank manager like me could have ended up with such an attractive and engaging woman like her. I thank my lucky stars every day for that woman."

"So how did you end up with her?"

"Your old man picked her up for me."

"What?" Josh laughed.

Hillman nodded. "We were having lunch at that deli around the corner from the bank and she was working there as a waitress. I had had my eye on her for months, but I could never work up the courage to ask her out. Your dad knew that, and to my great humiliation he waved her over to the table. He made a bet with her, and if he lost, he'd pay her a hundred bucks to have dinner with him."

"Huh? With him?"

"Screwy, right? I didn't get it either. And besides, your father was one good-looking guy. And he had that, you know, warm, easygoing air about him. He radiated confidence and charm. He was the most eligible bachelor in town, after all. So, yeah, I was pretty disappointed. I knew I couldn't compete with a guy like Taylor McCain."

"But you're married to her, so something went wrong...I mean right."

"Exactly. Your dad bet her that if she agreed to go out with me she'd have the absolute best date of her life, and that if she didn't he'd give her a hundred dollars and take her out himself. I was pretty pissed at him to tell you the truth, and as you might imagine, super embarrassed. I wanted to crawl under the table.

"Laura was put on the spot too, and I think she was mortified by his cocky complacency. But Taylor, always having been a good judge of character, had been counting on just that. He had figured that between my embarrassment and his smugness, she'd agree to the bet just to spite him. A good sport, Laura said, 'Okay, you're on. Looks like a win-win situation to me.'

"After we left I asked Taylor if he was out of his mind. I called him a prick. He just laughed. He saw that I was really nervous and told me not to worry; that he'd handle everything. I didn't know what he meant, but he came by my house that evening and planned the entire date out for me. He rented me a limousine, made reservations at the best restaurant in town, got me front row tickets to the theater, and rented me a tux. He sent her flowers, a bottle of fine champagne, and made sure that the doorman and owner of a great little jazz club in town knew I'd be stopping by. All on him. It didn't cost me a penny."

"Wow," Josh said, loving every minute of the story. It was a side of his father he never knew his dad possessed. "So, did she take the money or not?"

"Yeah, she did."

"No kidding?" Josh said. "That must have sucked."

"Not really."

"No?"

"Laura told him it was a good date, but not the best, and collected her hundred bucks from him. I sighed and told Taylor I was sorry I let him down, and that as far as I was concerned it was the best damn night of *my* life."

"I don't get it," Josh said. "I mean, you obviously saw her again."

Hillman grinned mischievously. "The very next weekend. Laura used Taylor's money for Yankees tickets, pizza, and beer. We had a big laugh and even more fun the second time around."

"You mean you were in on it! You guys cheated him!"

"Hey," Hillman laughed, "he deserved it. It wasn't until our wedding night did we tell Taylor what we had done."

"What did Dad say? Was he mad?"

"Hell, no. Not Taylor. He knew all along."

"He knew?" Josh said. "How?"

"He was at the game. He saw us! He sat ten rows behind us. He showed us a picture he had taken, and said that he had been waiting for the right time to show it to us. So he got the last laugh. Taylor always did. He was always one step ahead of the competition."

Hillman chuckled and shook his head with the memory. Josh saw that Hillman loved the story, and imagined he had told it a hundred times since. He had never seen Hillman this relaxed. Josh was happy that the man was enjoying himself. He was like another person, and Josh saw how a woman might actually like the guy. He had an infectious laugh and his eyes twinkled when he smiled. Josh just had never seen him smile or laugh before.

"Yep," Hillman said, "your dad was a great guy, one of a kind. A heart of gold. I miss him."

Josh nodded. "Yeah…"

"But I still haven't told you how he really changed my life."

"Tell me."

Hillman lowered his eyes and turned solemn. He said, "See, Laura and I had a son, Cal, and he died three years ago. He was only five. Leukemia. He was everything to us, and his death nearly destroyed me. I hit bottom: drinking heavily…the whole nine yards. My marriage and my job were hanging by a thread.

One night out of desperation I called your dad. Why him, I don't know. It was like a voice told me to.

"Taylor sensed something was seriously wrong and came right over. I swear, if he hadn't I would likely have done something really stupid that evening. I was a mess. He spent the entire night talking to me.

"But he didn't stop there. The next day, it was a Friday, he came by and told me to get in his car, that we were going for a ride. We went for a ride all right. He flew us to Montana for four days of fly fishing! He was in the middle of a multi-million dollar business deal, but he just left it all on hold so he could spend time with a loser like me. I was blown away by his kindness…"

Hillman spoke with a distant look in his eyes, as if he were watching Taylor cast his line into the river. He choked back his tears. "Blown away," he repeated, his voice cracking.

"I never knew you two were that close," Josh said. "I mean, he obviously considered you a very good friend."

"That's just it, Josh," Hillman said, "we weren't that close. We weren't pals. We were acquaintances, business associates. We saw one another maybe a couple of times a year, mostly business related stuff. When I say he changed my miserable life, I mean in a deeply profound way. He taught me the power of compassion. He taught me to never give up hope; never to think you are alone. He taught me that God never gives us a burden greater than we can carry."

"Wow," Josh said.

"You don't know the half of it. I returned from Montana a new man. Born again you might say. I cleaned up my act and nine months later Laura and I were gazing down in joy at a beautiful baby girl, Faith Taylor Hillman, the light of our lives. Had it not been for your dad, well, I don't even want to imagine it. Your father, by the way, lost that mega-million dollar deal to a competitor who didn't run off fly-fishing at the drop of a hat. I learned of it later through the grapevine and felt awful about it, thinking it was all my fault. I mentioned it to him the next time I saw him. He laughed and said he should be thanking *me*."

"Thanking you?"

"That's what I said. Ends up the company he had been in talks with had cooked their books. The IRS caught up to them, the company went bust, and their top management went to prison."

Josh turned pensive. "So, do you think...?" He paused.

Bob Hillman smiled wryly. "Think what?"

"Oh, nothing," Josh said.

"Do I think God works in mysterious ways?"

"Something like that, yeah," Josh said.

"I know a lot of people would call Taylor's goodwill and what resulted from it—saving all that time, money, and embarrassment—a coincidence or dumb luck."

"But not you," Josh said.

Hillman shook his head. "Not me, no. Although there was no one within twenty miles of that spot your dad and I were fishing at in Montana, we weren't alone. A wise silence pervaded all that beauty and stillness, and although I could never prove it, I believe we were in the presence of the Divine."

"You mean Nature, capital N?"

"If it makes you feel better," Bob Hillman said. "There's no denying the beauty and grandeur of the place. But neither I nor your dad would have been satisfied with such an explanation. For us, it was God." He grinned. "Capital G."

31

TELLING TIMES

*J*ust out of the shower, a towel around his waist, Josh ran his finger down the list. He tapped on each of two items:

- *Undo something that you've done.*
- *Finish a project worth starting.*

Pondering the two items, Josh walked to his window where he observed an elderly neighbor across the street watering his garden. He stared mesmerized at the rainbow created by the hose's mist in the morning light. Within the rainbow's arcing iridescence, Josh found his answer, and grinned.

The following day Josh spied Kyle backing out of his driveway and heading off to work. The coast clear, Josh stepped out from around the side of the house and strolled to the flower garden that he had destroyed doing his drunken *lambada* some two years earlier. He contemplated his handiwork. All that was left of the garden was a four-foot by eight-foot mound of weeds, crab grass, and Josh's fossilized footprints. He removed his daypack and pulled out gardening tools, seeds and some small plants, and got to work.

~

Josh stood in the center of the *dojo*. Three of Kazu's top students circled him. One by one they rushed at Josh. He dispatched each of them with a well-executed aikido move. Kazu nodded in approval, careful to conceal his immense pride.

When class was over and everyone had gone home, Josh and Kazu swapped places, and Josh took his turn as sensei. They sat back to back on the *dojo* floor, each holding a big, red plastic toy telephone that Josh had picked up for a buck at a garage sale.

"*Ding-a-ling-a-ling,*" Josh sang.

"*Hello?*"

"Hi. May I please speak with Mrs. Watanabe?"

"*I'm sorry, but she is not here. May I take a message?*"

"No, that's okay. I'll call back later."

"*Why?*"

"Pardon?"

"*Why?*" Kazu asked again. "*Who are you?*"

Josh grinned mischievously. "Well, if you must know, I am your wife's secret boyfriend."

"*Ah-so desu ka?*"

"That's right. Our destiny is to be together."

"*You believe in destiny?*" Kazu said. "*Show me your ugly face and I will introduce it to destiny.*"

"You will introduce me to your lovely wife, you cowardly little man?"

"*No, sir. I said to your destiny. It is a dark and kusai place!*"

"*Kusai?*" Josh said.

"*Um…bad smell?*"

"Oh, you mean stinky."

"*Yes, stinky place. Your destiny is stinky place in your butt where I will put your ugly face!*"

Josh cracked up laughing. "No, I'm sorry. You are wrong. My destiny is a beautiful place. At Keiko's side!"

"*You are a crazy man and my wife does not like crazy man.*"

"Men," Josh corrected.

"Men."

"Okay, tough guy. We shall see."

"We see what?" Kazu said.

"Time will tell."

Kazu checked his watch. "It's eight-thirty."

"Okay," Josh laughed. "I will see you in ten minutes."

"No, I am busy with English class. Come in twenty minutes."

"You study English?" Josh asked.

"Yes."

"Who is your teacher?"

"His name is Josh McCain."

"Is he a good teacher?"

"Yes, but he is crazy man like you."

"I see. Well, I'm not waiting twenty minutes. I'm coming over now."

"Now?"

"Right now!" Josh spun and grabbed Kazu in a bear hug. "Who you calling ugly?"

They rolled and wrestled and laughed across the *tatami*.

"Stinky place is coming to you!"

Josh sat on his window ledge and put his harmonica to his lips. He began to play. Within minutes all the neighborhood dogs started to howl. "All right all ready," he shouted. "Jeez, everyone's a critic."

He put down the harmonica and took up his knitting. It didn't take him long to lose himself in its meditative monotony. He mused over his recent lunch with Mr. Hillman, when suddenly he stopped, put down his knitting, and reached for a pen and yellow pad. He began scribbling away.

The next day he took his notes to the library and spent the morning typing at the computer. The words flowed from his fingertips. He returned every day for the rest of the week. Satisfied, Josh pedaled to the post office. He pulled a handful of large manila envelopes from his daypack and handed them over to the clerk, sending them on their way.

~

After leaving the post office, Josh decided to drop in on Berkowitz at the Sunny Day Senior Center for a few games of chess. He lost every game, but that he got Berkowitz to arch his bushy eyebrow a few times felt like the next best thing to victory.

Berkowitz had taken a liking to the young man, and little by little he opened the vast treasure chest of memories that his life contained. Between games he shared with Josh stories of his experiences growing up during the Great Depression, of the dozen different businesses he had started, and Josh's favorites, stories from the front lines in World War II, of D-day, and the Battle of the Bulge.

On this day Berkowitz pulled from his tweed coat pocket a small, polished oak chest. Inside were two Purple Hearts, two Bronze Stars, and a Silver Star.

"Berkowitz," Josh exclaimed. "You're a genuine hero!"

"I dunno," Berkowitz said. "I always believed that there were a lot of men far more heroic than me. Damn good men too. They just never lived to see the medals."

Josh gently picked up the Silver Star and weighed it thoughtfully in his hand. He looked up at the old man and tried picturing how he might have looked at nineteen.

"Thank you, Berkowitz," Josh said.

"For what? Teaching you chess? You stink."

Josh chuckled. "No," he said, holding up the star, "for all you did."

"Son, I got my thanks a hundred times over in ways you can't possibly know. I was there when we liberated Dachau. And take that bishop back, you knucklehead. You don't want to move there."

Josh smiled and handed Berkowitz back his medal, but Berkowitz held out his hand in rejection. "Keep it," he said.

"What?" Josh said, flabbergasted at the thought. "No way."

"Keep it. What am I going to do with it? I don't have anyone." He let out a little snort. "Well, a son somewhere teaching a load of rubbish in some fancy university, and he doesn't think much of soldierly things, if you catch my drift."

"Thanks," Josh said, "but I can't take it. I'm-I'm not... I know what this is, Berkowitz, and I'm not the kind of guy who should even be touching it."

"Listen, son, whoever you *think* you are, and whatever you *think* you've done, it is nothing compared to who you can be and what you can do if you set your mind to it. Where you have been is not half as important as where you are going. I suggest you learn this little lesson as fast as you can, because the longer you wait the harder it gets. The day when the scales tip and your past outweighs your future comes damn fast."

Berkowitz put his mottled hand over Josh's and rolled Josh's fingers into a fist around the Silver Star.

"Keep it," Berkowitz said solemnly. "If you don't think you're worthy, fine. Think of it as a spur in your dumb ass. I have faith in you, son. Maybe one day you'll put it on, and you'll feel nearly as proud as I did. Now, get that bishop out of the way of my knight and try challenging my crusty brain to fire up a few synapses for once, would ya?"

Josh smiled and pocketed the star. "Okay, you grumpy old fossil, no more Mr. Nice Guy." Josh moved his bishop and threatened Berkowitz's queen. "Take that!"

32

GHOSTO IN THE MACHINE

*W*earing sweats, muffler, and a woolen beanie over a pair of headphones, Josh passed off his quarter to Bagel Guy, and went long—but Bagel Guy's throw went longer. Josh put down his head and made a dash for the bagel. Unfortunately, the retinue of Hasidic Jews he often passed stood between him and the flying kosher doughnut. Josh saw them in the nick of time, and with Olympic-like dexterity, just avoided taking down the entire group in a thundering sprawl. Josh's acrobatics did not save him from colliding with one bearded old man, however, and he and Josh ended up staring at each other face-to-face on the ground, the old man on top, his large, round fur hat on Josh's chest.

"Are you okay?" Josh said. "I'm *so* sorry..." Josh handed the man his hat. "I didn't mean—"

"Rebbe!" exclaimed one of the entourage, a youth in black, horn-rimmed glasses, black hat, and long sidelocks, who rushed to the old man's aid and helped him up. The group scowled rebukingly at Josh.

"Sorry, sorry, *so* sorry," Josh repeated getting to his feet. Backpedaling, his hands in the air, bowing for forgiveness, he disappeared around the corner. Once out of sight of their scolding eyes, he let out a sigh of relief and shook his head. He took a bite from the bagel that he had miraculously caught, and continued his run.

When Brooke saw her nephew loping down the freshly snow-plowed street, she nearly spilled her morning latte on her lap.

"What the hell is he doing up at this hour?" she snarled to herself.

She pulled a U-turn and followed him until he vanished into the park. Parking a safe distance away, Brooke got out of her car. She looked on in surprise as Josh donned mittens, hopped onto the pull-up bars, and began whipping off pull-ups.

"Bad boy," she said, her eyes narrowed like peashooters. She snatched her cell phone from her purse and dialed Mr. Tweene.

Mr. Tweene fumbled in the darkness of his bedroom for his phone. *What SOB would be calling at this hour?* His cell phone read: Brooke Sievert. He groaned.

"Hello... Still? How is it poss—? ... Yeah, yeah... I under-stand. Don't worry, I'll handle it." Mr. Tweene clicked off and swung his legs over the side of the bed. "Bitch."

～

On his way home from his workout, Josh stopped by Kazu's garage. He knew Kazu would be up because he knew Kazu was an early-riser and enjoyed working on cars in the still hours of the morning before the interruptions began.

Josh slid open the garage door and greeted cheerfully, "Top of the morning to you, Kazu!"

Kazu had his head under the hood of a 1980 red Corvette. He looked up in surprise. "Good morning, Josh-san. Are you okay?"

"Yeah, fine. Great."

"It's early."

"The early bird catches the worm," Josh said.

"Worm?"

"You know—long, slimy, wiggly insect. Bird food."

Kazu frowned. "I am a worm?"

Josh chuckled. "Today you are. I have a favor to ask."

"What can a worm do for you?"

"I want to learn how to change the oil, battery, belts, and carburetor in a car."

"Why?"

"I just want to know how to do it, that's all."

Kazu gave him a queer look. "But Josh-san, you don't have a car."

"I used to."

"What kind?

"Porsche."

"You?!" Kazu said.

"Yeah."

"What happened?"

"I, um, lost it."

Kazu cocked his head in incomprehension. "How do you lose a car?"

"Actually, it was my dad's car."

"You lost father's Porsche?"

"Sorta, yeah."

"That's very bad, Josh-san."

"I didn't *really* lose it. He took it back. After he died."

"After he died? My English is very bad. You are saying to me ghosto took your car?"

"Sorta, yeah."

"Josh-san, you have big troubles."

"It's a long story."

"I like ghosto stories. Many Japanese believes in ghosto."

"It's not that kind of ghost, Sensei. Anyway, will you teach me? In exchange I'll help clean up around here or whatever. Anything."

"Okay. But you needs to come in morning before open. I'm busy after open."

"Fine. Great. Thanks, Sensei."

"And not every day. Mondays and Wednesdays are good."

"Okay, no problem."

"Why you wants to learn these things I still don't understand."

"If I learn how to do that stuff, I might get the car back."

"The ghosto said that?"

"Sorta, yeah."

Kazu shook his head. "Don't say to my wife why you come here."

"Why?"

"Keiko is afraid of ghosto."

Josh smiled. "Okay."

"And I want to drive your Porsche after you find it back," Kazu said.

"Get it back," Josh corrected.

"Get it back."

"Deal. But, to be honest, even if I learn how to do these things, I might not be able to get the car. I have to do many other things as well."

"What things?"

"Dance, run, play an instrument, knit a sweater, lots of things."

Kazu nodded. "Strange, Josh-san. Very strange."

"You don't know the half of it."

"It is not my business. My business is to be your friend. I will help you if I can."

"Thanks, Sensei. I appreciate it."

Kazu picked up a wrench and handed it to Josh. "I'm not afraid of ghosto," he said.

Josh smiled. "I'm sure you aren't."

"I'm not afraid of anything."

"I know, Sensei."

"Except Keiko sometimes," he said sheepishly.

Josh put his arm around Kazu's shoulder. "You're only human, Sensei."

"Yes," Kazu nodded. He pointed to where Josh was to apply the wrench. "Now turn this."

∼

Becky sat on Josh's lap as he read *Tom Sawyer* to her for the fourth time. Ms. Summers sat nearby engrossed in her macramé.

"'Now it's all done, Becky,'" Josh read, "'And always after this, you ain't ever to love anybody but me, and you ain't ever to marry anybody but me, ever never and forever. Will you?'"

A nurse entered and tapped Becky on the shoulder. "Okay, Becky, we're ready for you."

Becky groaned and turned to Josh. "Will you read to me in there, Josh? I have to know what Becky says!"

Josh laughed. "But you already know. This is the fourth time you've heard the story."

Becky rolled her eyes and said precociously, "Don't you know anything about women? She might change her mind this time!"

"Hmm," Josh said. "Maybe you're right. After all, that Tom is a very naughty boy."

"Very naughty," Becky agreed.

"So you don't want Becky to marry Tom?"

"I didn't say *that*."

"Oh, so you like naughty boys?" Josh teased.

"Well, I think if a naughty boy becomes a good boy he will be double good."

"Really? Who says so?"

"It's just my feeling."

Ms. Summers interrupted, "Becky, hurry on. The nurses are very busy and you are being rude. Josh will be there in a minute."

"Promise, Josh?" Becky pleaded.

"Promise, pumpkin."

Becky kissed him on the cheek and skipped away.

Josh turned to Ms. Summers. "Something the matter?"

Ms. Summers put aside her macramé and spoke frankly. "Becky's condition is fairly rare, Mr. McCain. It's usually elderly people who have to go on dialysis."

Josh grew suspicious. "I'm aware of that…"

"In the case of children," she continued, "dialysis can hinder maturation, resulting in stunted growth."

"What are you saying, that she'll end up a midget or something?"

"I'm saying that no one knows what the effects will be, but that she might not mature the way she was meant to."

"And there's nothing that can be done?"

"Outside of a kidney transplant, no."

"She's on some kind of donor waiting list, isn't she?"

"The best donor is a living relative, but I'm ineligible. Besides my age, we are ABO incompatible."

Josh turned pensive.

"However," she said, "I received a call yesterday from the donor bank, and they said that they found a compatible donor, but that we would have to act quickly."

"Great! What are we waiting for?"

"About $70,000, for starters."

"That much?"

"Then there are the drugs, immunosuppressives and the sort, and follow-up care…"

"Surely there are organizations, foundations, someone who can help."

Ms. Summers struggled to remain composed. "That all takes time, and like I said, we'd have to act quickly. The right donor is rare, and puberty isn't that far away. She may not get another chance."

Josh turned solemn and stared at the door marked, DIALY-

SIS. He stroked his chin in contemplation, and then turned back to Ms. Summers. "Do I have twenty-four hours?"

"What? What are you—?"

"Twenty-four hours. Okay?"

Ms. Summers fought tears of hope. "Do you really think…?"

"You just tell those donor people we want that kidney gift-wrapped." Josh turned and headed towards the dialysis room.

Ms. Summers called to him. "Mr. McCain…"

Josh turned and saw her moist, grateful eyes.

"If you can do this…" Her voice cracked and a tear ran down her cheek. "You're a saint."

"Believe me, Caroline, I'm no saint."

Josh turned and entered the dialysis room.

Becky smiled and waved. Josh held up his hands and demonstrated that they were empty. He closed them, rubbed one with the other, and—*poof!*—a Tootsie Pop appeared in his right hand. He waggled the candy teasingly in the air. Becky applauded and squealed with laughter.

33

GIRL TALK

*H*er Saturday shift over, Maggie waved goodbye to a group of nurses and made her way across the parking lot to her car. She was in a good mood. Tomorrow was a day off, and tonight she was meeting Josh. He had left a message on her phone saying that he was looking forward to seeing her; that he had something important to tell her. She wondered all day what that important thing might be, and replayed his words repeatedly in her head.

Was it bad? Was it good? He was "looking forward" to seeing me. If it were bad, he wouldn't have used that phrase, would he? No, that would be cruel. So, it must be something good, like...no, I'd better not get my hopes up. After all, if it were so good, why did he sound...? How did he sound? Distant? Not exactly. Fatigued, maybe? Distracted? Maggie shook her head. He's looking forward to seeing you, stupid, just leave it at that! You'll know in a few hours. Oh, that man drives me nuts! Why can't he just tell me little lies and try to get me into bed like a normal guy? Then, inserting her key into the door of her white Mustang, she realized what she had just thought, and chuckled. You are one confused girl, Maggie Ardor, she almost said aloud.

"We'll have to stop meeting like this," a voice said behind her.

Maggie turned and stood face-to-face with Brooke Sievert, who smelled of perfume and was dressed expensively, as if she were on the way to the theater. Maggie became instantly self-conscious. Still in her bland uniform, and having changed from her nurse's shoes to a pair of old sneakers, Maggie felt soiled and frumpy. She worried that she smelled of iodine, peroxide, and rubbing alcohol.

"Hello," Maggie said, smiling politely. "Yes, what a surprise."

"I saw you crossing the parking lot and just had to say hello."

"That's nice. Thank you."

"I haven't heard from my naughty nephew for quite awhile. I take it you have been keeping him pretty busy." She was all smiles.

"Oh," Maggie said good-naturedly, "he doesn't need me to keep busy. He seems to be able to stay pretty busy on his own, though I'm afraid I can't tell you exactly how."

"Can't or won't?" Brooke asked genially.

"Pardon?"

"You said he's very busy but you can't tell me about it."

"No," Maggie said, "I was making a little joke. I mean, yes, he seems to always be quite busy, but..."

"No need to explain, honey," Brooke said, waving her hand dismissively and smiling. "I know my Joshua. It's always some-thing with that boy. Or someone..." she said, letting the words trail off.

Maggie caught the drift, but let it pass. She didn't trust this Brooke woman, but she couldn't help but be curious about her either. Clearly, she and Josh had a history.

Brooke saw that she had Maggie's attention. "Will you be seeing Josh this evening?"

"Yes, I will."

"Please tell him I say hello."

"Of course."

"Has Josh taken you to Ciceroni's yet?"

"Where?"

"Ciceronis. His favorite Italian restaurant. *Very* romantic. Pricey, but he never seemed to mind. He and his friends often take their dates there."

"No," Maggie said. "We-we enjoy little cafes, window shopping, a movie now and then... I don't think Josh can afford such a dinner at the current time."

"Oh," Brooke said. "Sounds nice. Perhaps he should have practiced such simplicity with all his previous girlfriends."

"I..."

"Goodness," Brooke said, her hand flying to her mouth. "I just realized how awful that sounded. I'm so sorry. Please don't misunderstand me. I think it's wonderful that Josh doesn't feel he has to pretend with you."

"Pretend?"

"You know men," Brooke said, as if they were confidants. "Anything to get a girl into bed. Be it candle-lit dinners and a bottle of fine Merlot at a cozy Italian restaurant, or a pair of diamond earrings—whatever it takes."

"I'm sorry," Maggie said, "but I'm in a bit of a hurry and should be going now."

"Sure," Brooke said, extending her hand and shaking Maggie's, which was moist and limp. "It was so nice to see you again. Perhaps I can take you and Josh out for lunch one day?"

"Thank you, I'll mention it to Josh." She forced a smile and turned to her car. She didn't want Brooke to see her reddening eyes.

Maggie opened her car door and got in, but in her haste she smacked her prosthesis against the bottom of the car, creating a loud, dull-sounding—*thunk*. The bang only added to her humiliation. Maggie squeezed out another bent smile, and her eyes brimming, she started her car and backed away.

Brooke smiled innocently and waved.

34

HAVING GAME

*T*he full moon charged the blanket of snow on the park grounds with an iridescent blue hue. Josh and Maggie, dressed in winter jackets and scarves, sat on a seesaw slowly going up and down, their breaths trailing crystalline clouds in the night air.

"I haven't done this since I was a little girl," Maggie said. "Isn't that awful? I like seesaws. Why do we stop doing things we like in favor of so many things that we don't?"

"Habit, I guess," Josh said.

"When was the last time you came to the park?" she asked.

"Five this morning."

Maggie smirked. "Liar."

"Really."

"You did? Why?"

Josh grinned. "Habit."

"You come here *every* morning?"

"Did."

"And it never occurred to you to mention such a thing to me? Exactly how nutty are you?"

"It was just a phase."

"Waking at dawn and marching out into the freezing cold

when you don't have to is not a phase. It's a sign of a loose screw." She added with a smile, "Or maybe a bag of them."

"Yeah, so it would seem. Anyway, I left a message on your machine that I had something I wanted to tell you."

"And I've been worried all day because of it, thank you very much."

"I want to say that I'm sorry that I've been less than scarce these past months. And that, well, from now on I'm going to be around a lot more. If it's okay with you…"

"With me? You mean you weren't spending all that time with…other friends?"

"No."

"You *do* have other friends, right?"

"Sure."

"Can I meet them?"

"I guess. Why not?"

Maggie sniffed. "How inviting."

But Josh was too distracted by his own thoughts to hear her, and his absence only verified for Maggie the sources of the insecurities she was feeling. They seesawed up and down in silence for a minute, both lost in their own divergent thoughts.

Maggie broke the silence. "Are you ashamed of me, Josh?"

"What? No. Don't be ridiculous."

"Then why haven't you ever asked me out?"

"What do you mean? We've been out tons of times, and besides, like I said, from now on things are going to be different." Josh swept his hand gesturing to the snowy park around them and smiled brightly. "And look, we're out now."

"Oh yes, ten o'clock in a frozen, deserted park where no one can see us."

"It's romantic," Josh said, hoping a little simple-minded jesting would ease whatever was bugging her.

Maggie stopped the seesaw, parking Josh in the air.

Uh-oh.

"So is wearing a nice dress and eating out at a fine restaurant, one with a pretty candle on the table and maybe a glass of Merlot. You have never even tried to kiss me at the door! It's me, I know it. I've always known it."

"Whoa, Maggie, calm down. It's not you. It's—"

"Don't you dare say it!"

"Say what?"

"I'll scream, I swear."

"Maggie?"

"'It's not you, Maggie, it's me.' Are you that spineless? Oh, and of course you hope to remain friends, right? Well, I don't need another friend, Josh. Unlike you, I have many friends. To hell with you and all the others just like you!" Maggie leaped from the seesaw, sending Josh crashing to the ground.

"Ow!"

"You don't know what you want. And you don't know what you had!"

"Maggie—"

"I can't believe I...I'm so stupid." Maggie broke into tears and ran hobbling off, tripped, and fell face first into the shallow snow.

"Maggie!" Josh sprang up and raced towards her.

Maggie clambered to her feet, weeping in anger and humiliation. "Stay away from me!" she commanded, her arm stretched out before her.

Josh halted.

"And stay away from Becky too!" She turned and ran off in tears.

Josh called after her. "Maggie!"

She scampered on without looking back, slipping and nearly falling again.

Josh sighed. "Oh Maggie..."

He wondered if he should just suck it up and go after her; chase her down and...what? She clearly was in no mood for a rational discussion. Whatever was eating her was more than he could handle. He even worried that if he ran up to her she might whip around and slap him or something, and he didn't want to deal with *that*.

She was usually so levelheaded. Why couldn't she have just lectured him like before? That went well. He rubbed his bum, which still smarted from his crash. *What did I say, anyway?* He thought he was telling her that he wanted to spend more time with her, that he really looked forward to it, then the next thing he knew—anger, crashing, and tears. *Man...*

Maggie's train of thought was far less contiguous. She had blown an emotional gasket, and she found herself in the dark hugging a tree and bawling her eyes out. She couldn't think; she could only cry. She didn't know why she had exploded so, but didn't dare pursue the thought. It was too painful. For now, sobbing would have to do.

She loved him. She loved him more than anyone she'd ever known, and it scared her to death. He would never love her back; never take her love seriously. In an emotional spasm, she said, "Forget him. Just forget him!"

Worried for her safety, Josh went looking for Maggie, pleadingly calling out her name. Then he heard the unmistakable sound of Maggie's Mustang starting up. He was relieved. At least she was safe.

Halfway home Josh decided that he wanted a beer. He hadn't had one in many months, but he was going to have one now.

Outside the *Time Out Bar and Grill*, Mr. Tweene handed Mick another envelope. He poked Mick in his bright orange ski vest, making a point. "And this time," Tweene said, "leave his pecker standing so Candy's got something to sit on."

"If you want the twerp out of commission why can't I just, you know, break his arm or somethin'? Why does she have to do anything with him? It's weird, man."

"Because, you oaf, that means questions and questions mean

snoopy people. Cops and lawyers. We can't have that. She's just acting, all right?" He patted his camera. "She knows she doesn't have to go farther than a little smooching." Tweene grinned. "… If she doesn't want to. Don't get all bent out of shape. Now get going." Mr. Tweene pushed Mick towards the door.

Inside the bar, an eight ball dropped into a corner pocket. Solids covered the pool table. Leaning across the table, cue in hand, was Candy. Her shapely buns poised in the air, the sculptured masterpiece held the gawping attention of every guy within eyeshot.

She stood, snapped her fingers, and opened her palm for payment. "Like taking candy from a baby," she said.

"Nice game," Josh said, slapping a five into her hand.

"You flatter yourself," Candy said.

A heavy paw dropped onto Josh's shoulder and spun him around. "You got balls showing your face around here again," Mick growled.

"Hey! … Oh, hi, Mick. Can I buy you a beer? I think we got off on the wrong foot the las—"

Mick shoved Josh in the chest and sent him backpedaling towards a red brick wall.

Josh said, "You're gonna beat my face in again, aren't you?"

Mick pushed him again. "For starters, yeah, and this time you don't have your taco-bending friend to help you."

"Um, he's Japanese, Mick, not Mexican."

"Same thing, asshole."

"Mick, listen. If I told you that I've had a rough day, and that an hour ago the best thing that ever happened to me never wants to see me again, would that change your mind?"

Mick glanced at Candy and suppressed his jealousy. "Not in the least," he snarled.

He knocked Josh again, driving him within a few feet of the wall. A number of regulars circled around and egged Mick on.

"Okay, Mick, if it's that important to you, then let's get it over with." Josh cupped his hands to his mouth and appealed to the barroom. "Would someone please call an ambulance?" He turned to Mick, shrugged, and dropped his hands to his sides in surrender. "Just trying to save some time."

"Smartass…"

Mick swung, but Josh parried and locked up Mick's arm. In the same fluid movement, Josh dragged the big man down in a whirling circle, and slammed him headfirst into the brick wall—introducing him, as Kazu was fond of saying, to his own stupidity. Mick slumped to the ground unconscious.

The barroom went silent.

Josh lifted his jacket off a hook on the wall and strolled towards the door.

Candy ran up to Josh and hooked her arm in his. "Nice," she purred.

Josh grinned. "Like taking Candy from a baby?"

He unhooked his arm and flashed his hand twice. Magically, a Tootsie Pop appeared. He handed it to Candy.

"Or not," he said, and strolled triumphantly out the door.

35

SACRIFICE

*J*effrey Barnes, Wayne Powers, Chad Jefferson, and Brooke Sievert sat around the conference table at McCain Industries. Powers and Chad were immersed in a game of chess.

Chad sneezed and shot Brooke an accusing eye. "You wore that bug spray again on purpose, didn't you?"

Brooke smirked.

They heard a knock at the door and automatically checked the clock to see how late Josh was this time. They exchanged looks of surprise—9:55?

Powers said snidely, "He hocked his watch so he probably doesn't even know he's early."

Josh strolled in, dressed in jeans, sneakers, and a wrinkled white oxford: a far cry from the comical hodgepodge of his earlier visit some sixteen months before. He extended his hand to Mr. Barnes.

"Hello, Jeffrey. Long time no see."

Josh acknowledged the others. "Wayne ... Chad ... Brooke. Thanks for coming." Josh took a seat at the table.

Jeffrey Barnes said, "What can we do for you, Josh?"

"I've come to ask for the two-hundred thousand that you

mentioned." He nodded to Brooke. "The rest is all yours, Brooke."

Brooke hitched one of her well-manicured eyebrows and struggled to suppress her glee. Well, well, she thought, that loser Tweene finally came through.

Barnes slid a check across the table to Josh. "Two-hundred-thousand dollars," he said.

Josh wondered if Barnes was going to reenact the same game he played the last time he slid a paper across the table, but Barnes withdrew his hand. No more games. Josh looked at the check, smiled, and put it into his wallet.

"You were all expecting this, obviously," Josh said.

"We're just wondering what took you so long," Barnes said. "You should have been back over a year ago. Your tardiness cost me fifty bucks."

"You bet on me?"

"Against you," Barnes said.

Josh grinned. "You should know better than to bet against a McCain. Which one of you pocketed the money?"

Barnes and Powers tossed a glance over at Chad Jefferson.

"Chad? Thanks! Hey, you wouldn't consider applying some of that fifty towards new curtains for the old place, would you?"

"Fat chance," Chad said, unamused. "When are you moving out?"

"I'm not. I mean, if that's okay with you."

Chad was taken by surprise. Why, he wondered, would the boy want to keep living in such a dump when he had two-hundred grand in his pocket? He said, "As long as you keep up on your rent, why should I care?"

"I appreciate it, Chad. Thank you."

An uncomfortable silence descended upon the room. The three friends weren't expecting such a disarming Josh.

"Well," Josh said, "guess I'd better be going. Take care, guys." He stood to leave.

Chad said to Powers, "Your move."

Powers returned his attention to the chess game. Josh strolled over and stood between the two men and looked on. Chad and Powers glanced up at him, annoyed. Powers examined the chessboard, and moved his knight.

Josh said, "You don't want to do that."

"I do," Powers growled.

"Not really…" Josh took the knight back and moved up one of Power's pawns.

Powers was about to protest when he noticed that Chad had taken a deep interest in Josh's move. Chad countered.

Josh stroked his chin, and moved Powers' bishop. Chad narrowed his concentration. He took his turn, capturing Power's rook. Chad smirked in satisfaction.

"Dios mío!" Josh said. "Sorry, Wayne."

Powers rolled his eyes, unamused.

Josh moved Power's knight and turned to leave. "Thanks a lot guys, really." He strolled whistling out of the room.

Powers snorted and returned to the game. He was about to demand that he be able to take back the past few moves when he noticed Chad's furled brow.

"Son of a —" Chad said, impressed. "Checkmate, pal. You win."

"Huh?" Powers said. He examined the board. Chad was right. Checkmate.

Chad cast an inquisitive eye towards the door as it closed with a gentle *click*. He grinned.

That evening Josh stood bare-chested in front of the bathroom mirror brushing his teeth, lost in thought. He glanced at the list beside the mirror. More than half of the items had been crossed off. Each item represented a story, a person, and a hundred different memories.

He checked his physique in the mirror and flexed like a body builder, his toothbrush dangling from his mouth. He hadn't really looked at himself for many months and was surprised by what he saw.

"Man," he garbled, "I'm ripped." He flexed some more, and chuckled. "Cool."

Josh spat, rinsed, and then took the list from the wall and walked with it into the other room. After contemplating it one last time, he dropped it into the wastepaper basket. The list floated downward like a leaf, and landed face up in the basket. He turned off the light, crawled into bed, and stared at the ceiling.

36

THAT'S RIFE

*J*osh and Kazu held the day's English lesson on the steps just outside the *dojo*.

Josh thought Kazu could use some work on his pronunciation, especially with L and R, which, being Japanese, were particularly difficult letters for Kazu to pronounce. Mere repetition wasn't working too well, so Josh hit on the idea of singing *Row Your Boat*, hoping a little melody might help. Josh sang first, and then Kazu followed the best he could:

"*Row, row, row your boat...*"

"*Low, low, low your boat...*"

"*Gently down the stream...*"

"*Gentry down the stream...*"

Meanwhile, in the hospital operating room, Becky was undergoing her kidney transplant. Maggie, in scrubs and a mask, assisted. She handed an instrument to the operating surgeon, and then rubbed a joyful tear away with her shoulder.

"*Merrily, merrily, merrily, merrily...*"

"Merriry, merriry, merriry, merriry," struggled Kazu.

"Life is but a dream."

"Rife is but a dream."

The two busted out laughing and Josh gave Kazu the thumbs up.

~

Josh, a Teddy Bear under his arm, strolled into Becky's hospital room. The door was open and Ms. Summers, who sat at Becky's bedside, didn't see Josh enter. The little girl was hooked to an IV and other instruments, but sleeping soundly.

Josh saw that Ms. Summers was reading the Bible. He made his presence known by softly reciting Psalm 23:

"'The Lord is my shepherd; I shall not want. He maketh me to lie down in green pastures; He leadeth me beside the still waters. He restoreth my soul; He leadeth me in the paths of righteousness for His name's sake. Yea, though I walk through the valley of the shadow of death, I will fear no evil; for Thou art with me; Thy rod and Thy staff they comfort me...'"

Josh smiled at his moist-eyed friend, and winked.

Ms. Summers smiled back. "My, my, Mr. McCain, I would never have taken you as a Bible-quoting fellow."

"Memorizing stuff used to be a hobby of mine. How about this one? 'There once was a man from Nantucket, whose—'"

Ms. Summers swatted her bony hand at the raunchy limerick. "You're awful," she chuckled.

"How's she doing?" Josh asked.

"Good. The doctor said everything went very smoothly."

"That's great." Josh pulled an envelope from his back pocket and handed it to Ms. Summers. "A banker friend of mine, a Mr. Hillman, helped me set up a trust fund for Becky that ought to cover her for some time to come. We'll need your signature."

She took the envelope and opened it. Her eyes ballooned in

astonishment. "Mr. McCain, how on earth did you ever raise such a large sum of money? And so quickly?"

"Where there's a will there's a way, Caroline. Isn't that the saying?"

"You didn't do anything…stupid, did you?"

"Nothing illegal, anyway, if that's what you're getting at."

"Well, thank you, Mr…Josh. I simply don't know—"

Maggie, clipboard in hand, entered the room. "What's he doing here?" she asked Ms. Summers.

Josh answered by waving the Teddy Bear. He set it down beside Becky.

Maggie contemptuously ignored him and began looking after Becky. She stroked the sleeping girl's hair and kissed her tenderly on the forehead.

Josh looked on, touched by Maggie's display of affection.

"Caroline," Maggie said businesslike as she attended to Becky, "I need the address to the 'mysterious institution' you say made this miracle possible. I want to write them a grateful letter." The Teddy Bear in her way, Maggie threw it brusquely aside.

Josh cleared his throat. "I have something for you too, Maggie." He pulled a second envelope from his pocket and offered it to her.

Maggie squinted at him, hesitated, and then took the envelope. She withdrew a handmade invitation card.

You are cordialy invited to attend a dinner party at the home of Kyle Dressler to be hosted by one Joshua McCain in the honor of one Maggie Ardor.

   Formal wear required.
   When: Friday, May 12th, 7:00 p.m.

"Cordially has two L's," Maggie said tartly.

"Does that mean you won't come?"

"Who's Kyle?"

"My best friend."

"My honor?"

"Yeah."

"Why? What kind of joke—?"

Ms. Summers snatched the card away and read it. Irritated, she said, "Oh, for goodness sakes, woman." She turned to Josh. "Of course she's going." She shot Maggie a stern, rebuking eye.

"Okay then," Josh said. "I have to run. Caroline, please tell Becky I'll be back later with some ice cream, okay?"

As soon as Josh was out the door, Ms. Summers turned to Maggie and popped her on the forehead with Josh's envelope.

"What?" Maggie said.

Ms. Summers snorted in disgust. "Romance is wasted on the young."

"Caroline, he's a creep."

"Yes, well, don't forget to mention that in your 'grateful' letter to him." She slapped the envelope containing the trust into Maggie's hand.

"Him? What are you talk—?"

Ms. Summers, arms folded, nodded smugly as Maggie opened the envelope and began reading about the trust fund.

The revelation sank in. "Oh my...*Josh?*"

37

BULLETPROOF

Friday, May 12
"Do good by stealth, and blush to find it fame."
— Alexander Pope (1688-1744), English Poet

*T*he interior of Kyle Dressler's upscale suburban home had the look of someone who was trying to be sophisticated but couldn't quite be rid of his college days. Pricey modern art hung on one living room wall; and on the other, cheap, unframed movie posters. But his fiancé's touch could already be seen taking over, as the new furniture, plush carpeting, and stone-tiled floors attested. The movie posters' days were numbered, and everyone but Kyle seemed to know it.

Kyle, Shelly, Maggie, Kazu, and his Japanese-American wife, Keiko, a tiny woman with doe-like eyes, shiny black hair, and a pearly smooth complexion, sat around Kyle's dining room table, cheerily chatting and sipping a fine California Merlot. They had just finished eating, and empty dishes spoke of a multi-coursed feast. The men wore tuxes and the women evening gowns.

Shelly said, "What on earth is Josh doing in there?"

"I think I'll check if he needs a hand," Maggie said. She

started to get up, but just then Josh, dressed in a fifties-era tux, entered holding a flaming dessert. Everyone *oohed* and *ah'd*.

"Watch out," Josh said, "this thing might explode."

Kyle said, "Josh McCain putting together a seven course meal? Who'd have thunk it?"

"Thunk?" Kazu said, confused. "Isn't it, thought?"

"Pay no attention to my ignorant friend," Josh replied, setting the dessert in front of Shelly. "He thinks participles are something you put on a pizza."

Kazu scratched his head.

"Josh," Shelly exclaimed. "This looks divine. Where did you learn to cook like this?"

"Alfonso is teaching me. Hold the compliments until after you've tasted it. I hope you've all paid your health insurance premiums." Josh disappeared back into the kitchen.

"Who's Alfonso?" Kyle asked.

"He owns the restaurant Jozy works at," answered Maggie.

"Jozy?"

Maggie chuckled. "That's what Alfonso calls him. We're not sure if he does it on purpose or not."

"Josh works in a restaurant? As what," Kyle said snidely, "a busboy?"

"And dishwasher and waiter," Maggie rejoined. "He does it all."

Kyle and Shelly exchanged bemused glances. "Well," Shelly said, "Jozy is full of surprises, though normally not this pleasant."

"Shelly," Kyle said, "don't go ruining Maggie's image of Josh. Let him do that himself."

"Oh, believe me," Maggie said, "I have no illusions about that man. He has trouble written all over him."

Everyone at the table laughed, except Kazu, who didn't understand their sarcasm, and so felt compelled to stick up for his friend.

"You people know Josh-san long time. Your eyes see him

with many years of memory. Memory is powerful filter. My eyes have no memory."

"People change, is that what you're saying, Kazu?" Maggie asked.

Kazu shook his head. "Most people don't change ever. They think they change, but it is only opinions they change. They change clotheses or hairstyle, but not self. Sleeping people dream of change; awakening people change their dreams."

Josh returned with a stack of dishes and started handing them out. He became aware that everyone was staring at him.

"What?" he said. "Hey, I was kidding about the insurance, okay?" He shook his head and handed Shelly a big knife to do the honors.

They finished the evening with more wine, coffee, and a short video Kyle shot of his and Shelly's recent trip to the Bahamas. Afterwards, they took their farewells outside. Kazu and Keiko thanked their hosts profusely and were first to leave. Josh and Maggie lingered a little longer.

Maggie and Shelly chatted together across the driveway opposite the men. "I must say," Shelly said, "Josh certainly seems a different man since he met you."

"This is pretty much how I found him," Maggie said.

"You found him in the hospital beaten to a pulp."

"Yes, but—"

"Hey," Shelly said quickly, "forget I said anything. It looks like he had some sense knocked into him, and that's what counts."

Maggie shrugged, perplexed. "Well, thanks again, Shelly, for a wonderful evening."

"I didn't do a thing. Thank Josh there."

Maggie sighed. "I would if he'd let me…"

"Oh come on—"

Maggie nodded dismally. "Would you believe I've never even

been to his apartment?"

"No. ... Really?"

Maggie continued to nod in dreary affirmation. "The man has never laid a lip on me."

"Wow. Now *that* is strange."

"So it is me!"

"No, no. I mean, it's just—shit."

Josh and Kyle stood beside Kyle's blooming garden. Josh gestured towards the ladies with his chin. "What do you think Shelly is saying?" he asked.

"Aw, I'm sure she's putting a good word in for you. Maggie is the first girl you ever dated that Shelly didn't want to punch. So, hey," he said, giving Josh a chummy slap on the shoulder, "tonight was about having blown off my engagement party, wasn't it?"

"Come on, Kyle, you know I'd never be so obvious."

"Yeah, you're not that cool. Now listen, I'm only mentioning it once, and you'll be getting the invitation in the mail, but our wedding is on September 15th. Got it?"

"What took so long? You've been engaged for a year and a half."

"My work, then her work, then my work, then—but it doesn't matter. September 15th, and that's a definite go. Be there or be dead, 'cuz you're my best man."

"Me?"

"You."

"After all I did, didn't do, almost did, and almost didn't do?"

"Yeah, well don't rub it in," Kyle said.

"September 15th? That's one day after—"

"After what?"

"Nothing," Josh said. "It doesn't matter anymore."

"What doesn't—?" And then Kyle began to nod. "Oh-h right, the fiendish list. That's the two year deadline, isn't it?"

The Will

"Was, yeah."

"I *knew* you took the money."

"How? Did Chad or one of the other guys tell you?"

"We lawyers, we're like detectives, man. How else could a busboy have afforded a tux?"

"Nice try, Sherlock, but I borrowed it from a guy named Berkowitz."

"So what did you do with the money? I mean, two-hundred grand, that's no chump change."

"Let's just say I had a lot of bills that needed paying," Josh said.

"What a waste, eh?"

Josh shrugged. "Nah, not really. I was just glad I could take care of them."

"Listen, buddy," Kyle said. "Don't feel too bad about giving up on that list. I mean, it was the fricking twelve labors of Hercules times three. Nobody could do all the crap that was on that list—not in two years, not in five years, and especially not you."

"What do you mean, especially not me?"

"Dude, you're Josh."

"Yeah, so?"

"Josh, man," Kyle repeated.

"Yeah, so?"

"Josh," Kyle explained again.

"I heard you the first time, Kyle." He looked over at Maggie. "Anyway, it's time to move on."

Kyle followed Josh's gaze. "Not that you need my approval or anything, but I like her. She's not your type."

Josh chuckled. "Thanks."

"Pretty too," Kyle said.

Josh nodded. *"And* very punctual."

Kyle lowered his voice. "But I thought you were…you know, a leg man."

Josh said coolly, "And I thought you used to have some class."

"Hey, come on," Kyle said. "Those were your own words not so long ago."

"Yeah, well, just because I used to be an idiot doesn't mean you have to take over the job."

"I didn't mean anything, you know that. It's just you're not—"

"Not what?" Josh said.

"I guess a lot can happen in a year and a half, that's all."

"Nothing just happens in this life, Kyle. Everything has reason and consequence. Everything. At least if you're alive it does."

"Yeah, all right, Socrates. So what's the reason you...?"

Kyle saw that Josh had tuned him out and was staring across the way at Maggie. She was laughing at something Shelly had said, and Kyle recognized a profound fondness in Josh's smile. Kyle smirked and launched into Cat Stevens' classic song "Hard-headed Woman."

"I'm lookin' for a hardheaded woman, headed woman..."

"What?" Josh said, snapped from his trance.

"Someone who'll make me do my be-e-est..."

"I get it, Kyle."

"And if I find—"

"Yo!"

"Hardheaded Woman, dude. Every existentially-alienated loner's theme song."

"The existentialists were a bunch of tedious narcissists. And I'm not lonely."

"Where the fuck did you get all those syllables?" Kyle snorted. "And the hell you aren't. I'm your only friend, and I haven't seen you for over a year, you prick."

"You talk to your mother with that mouth, Kyle? And I hate to break the news to you, old buddy, but I have lots of friends." He named them off on his fingers. "I got Kazu, Alfonso, Blues Man, Bagel Guy, Mummy Man, Berkowitz—"

Kyle busted out laughing. "Dude, it sounds like the makings

of a comic strip—the Dork League!"

"Yeah, well, remember your roots, Kyle. You were the biggest dork around until I took you under my cape."

"You got a point there. Why did you anyway?"

"I don't know, but maybe inside every cool guy like me is a nerd struggling to get out."

Kyle laughed and slugged Josh playfully in the stomach. "Dude!" Kyle exclaimed, impressed. "Where'd the Teddy-belly go?" He punched Josh again—hard. "Ow," he squealed, shaking the hurt from his wrist.

"Hey, hey," Shelly said walking up with Maggie. "No roughhousing."

"Shelly," Kyle said, "check out Josh's bulletproof abs. Go on, hit him. Hit him as hard as you can."

Shelly rolled her eyes. "Grow up, Kyle."

Maggie said, "I'm sorry everyone, but I have to be at work in six hours."

"Sure," Josh said. "Let's go. Talk to you guys later."

"Thanks again," Maggie said. "I had a wonderful time."

"Don't be strangers," Kyle said.

Josh and Maggie walked away towards Maggie's car.

"Poor girl," Shelly said. "She's doomed."

"I don't know," Kyle said, still rubbing the hurt from his wrist.

"C'mon, Kyle. It's Josh. The same guy who demolished your garden." Shelly pointed at the garden, which looked better than ever. "When do you find the time to work on it, anyway? I've never seen you touch it."

"I never told you?" Kyle said. "It was the weirdest thing. I received a letter from an old client of mine who said he got me a year's gardening service as a belated engagement present. But I have no idea which client—no name, nothin'. The gardener comes while I'm at work. Mows the grass and everything. Cool, huh?" He put his arm around Shelly and they walked towards the door. "See," he said, "not *everyone* hates lawyers."

38

PAPER CHAINS

*M*aggie pulled up in front of Josh's apartment building and turned off the ignition.

"Aren't you going to invite me up?" she asked.

"No."

"Why not?"

"Because you have to be at work in six hours."

"No, I don't. I lied. I switched shifts with someone. Besides, according to Shelly, luring women up to your apartment has never weighed particularly heavy on your conscience."

"Shelly," Josh groaned. "It's just that—" He broke into a roguish smile. "Wait—no, it's not. Not anymore."

"Huh?"

Josh snatched Maggie's keys from the ignition and bounded out of the car. He headed up the walk dangling her keys above his head.

Josh hit the lights and opened his arms in presentation of his apartment.

"How…bohemian," Maggie said.

"Believe me, it looked a lot worse when I moved in."

Maggie began a desultory look around. She picked up Josh's harmonica from on top of the dresser.

"Can you play it?" she asked.

"Ask the neighborhood dogs. They're always howling for an encore." Josh gestured toward the bathroom. "Excuse me a minute..." He walked into the bathroom and closed the door.

Maggie continued her tour. She noted the many books laying around and the quotes and poems taped to the walls. With amusement she picked up and examined his knitting, which she presumed was the beginning of a sweater. She continued her snooping when her prosthetic bumped into the wastepaper basket, knocking it over. Bending to pick up the litter, she spotted Josh's list.

Inside the bathroom, Josh flushed the toilet, grabbed his toothbrush and paste, and began a frenzied brushing. His eyes wandered to where the list used to be. Free at last, loins in a stir, he grinned and brushed faster.

Josh opened the door and saw Maggie standing beside his bed, her hands behind her back. She smiled coquettishly and flashed her bedroom eyes. Barely able to contain his excitement, Josh beelined it to the light switch by the door.

"It's been a long time, Josh," Maggie cooed.

"Don't worry. Gentle Josh, that's me..."

Josh hit the lights and the room went black.

"I'm not talking about me," Maggie said, silhouetted by the darkness.

"Huh?"

"What," she guessed, "about a year and a half?"

Josh switched the light back on.

Maggie waved the list and squinted at Josh's undone belt and pants. "Buckle up, buster," she commanded. "You have some explaining to do."

Hours later, dawn spilling over the rooftops, Josh and Maggie sat facing each other on the window ledge sipping coffee.

"I still don't know why you couldn't tell me," Maggie said.

"There were lots of reasons."

"Name one."

"Okay, say I didn't take the money. Say I actually finished the list and –"

"You thought I'd only be interested in the money?" Maggie said, offended.

"Come on, it was a lot of money. A *lot* of money. If it were you…?"

"If it were me?" she said resentfully. "If it were me…?"

"Yeah?"

Maggie smiled, disarmed. "I'd never have gotten half as far through that list as you did."

"Huh?"

"No way. I'm angry, yes, but not nearly as angry as I am proud. No, awed."

"Really?"

She nodded. "You put into action the sort of thing I could only fantasize about. The *will*, Josh. Not the paper one, the real will. You met it, embraced it—and you learned what it can do. I envy you, Joshua McCain. And perhaps the only person I admire more than you is your father who loved you this much."

Josh looked into Maggie's big brown eyes, and blinked. Although she hadn't slept for almost twenty-four hours, to Josh, Maggie never looked more beautiful. Her sleeveless, tapered satin blue dress showed off the contours of her body, and her tresses of wavy black hair draped about her smooth shoulders and chest, perfectly framing her pretty, dimpled face.

Josh glanced out the window and sipped his coffee. He reflected upon the tranquility of the early morning street. He thought of Bagel Guy making his rounds. He wondered if his morning pal would miss him.

"Yeah, well, it's over."

"No, it's not," Maggie said.

"Yo, selective-memory-girl. I took the money, remember? It's over."

"Not while I'm your girl, it's not."

"What are you talking about?"

"I'm saying, I don't think it's about the money, Josh. I think somewhere along the line all these crazy things your dad made you do, they unearthed something deep and authentic in you, and it became about something else."

"Like what?"

"Aretê." Maggie slapped the list down on Josh's lap. "Look, all these peculiar things, there's a method to this madness."

"What do you mean?"

"Well, I was looking at the list, and it struck me that all these efforts seem to fall into three groups—mind, body, and spirit. You said your dad admired the ancient Greeks and fancied himself a philosopher of sorts, right?"

"I guess. So?"

"Well, isn't that what the Greeks aimed for, *aretê?* Excellence —a sound mind in a sound body?"

"You're saying my dad was a nutcase?"

"I'm saying he believed in you, Josh. And so do I."

Josh wagged his head. "Maggie, I'm not anything remotely—"

"No, you listen. I don't know the old Josh, but I know the real Josh, and that's all I'll ever need to know, okay? And you know what else I know?"

Josh shook his head, speechless.

"You're going to finish that list. On time. Every single item on it."

"What? You've got to be joking!"

Maggie shook her head.

"Why?" he said. "What for?"

"For the man in you who is waiting across that finish line."

"But—"

"And for me," she added.

"What could completing the list possibly have to do with you?"

Maggie looked beseechingly into Josh's eyes, wanting desperately for him to understand. "Don't you see? Completing that list means anything is possible. It means the chains that bind us —our mistakes, the past, bad luck, fate—they are all frauds. They are all just paper chains."

Maggie's eyes pooled as she took his hands pleadingly in hers.

"I want to believe, Josh. I want so badly to believe that within each of us is a reservoir of untapped freedom and will, and that anyone—even I—can find it too. But I'm weak. I haven't the faith I wish I had. I need to see it with my own eyes. Show it to me, Josh. Show me that it's true."

"Maggie, come on; you're the hero, not me. You're on the front lines of life sixty hours a week dealing with things most of us hope never to see. You save lives and demonstrate more kindness and patience in a week than most people do in a lifetime. What I've done is nothing—it's *squat*."

"No, Josh. I cope. I make the best of bad situations. Millions do it every day, and better than I. What you are doing is different. Your father launched you on an amazing adventure that has taken you to people and places and things you never dreamed about before. He knew it would, I'm sure of it. And, he brought you to me. I can't do what you can, but I can help you. Let me help you, Josh."

39

MOJO RISING

*C*had Jefferson climbed the stairs to Josh's apartment, a set of new curtains draped over his arm. As he ascended, he heard the sound of someone playing a harmonica. It grew louder as he neared Josh's door. He raised his hand to knock, and then paused. He put his ear to the door and listened. On second thought, he laid the curtains in front of the door and walked away.

On his way out, he saw the mailman in the foyer slip three identical-looking envelopes into Josh's box. Chad waited on the stairs, and when the coast was clear, he opened Josh's mailbox and pulled out the self-addressed envelopes. One of them hadn't been properly sealed and he was able to open it without tearing. Inside was a form letter:

Dear Mr. McCain,

Thank you for your interest in Executive Magazine. We are sorry to inform you that your article "Where There's a Will There's a Way: The Story of Taylor McCain" is not the type of story we are accepting at this time. We wish you better luck elsewhere.

Chad cast a surprised, reflective eye back up the stairs.

~

"I don't think I can do this, Blues Man," Josh said nervously. "I'm not nearly ready."

"We ain't never really ready for nothin' in this life, my man," Blues Man said. "If we was, what need would there be for blues music?" He smiled big, his great, white teeth reflecting the bright lights they were standing beneath. Four of Blues Man's buddies strolled up, all white-haired old-timers like himself.

"Okay, fellas," one said. "Let's shake the rust and show these fine folks that we still got some."

Another said to Josh, "You're gonna be fine, kid. Just let the ole mojo do its thing."

The six of them walked out onto the darkened stage and took their positions behind a drawn curtain. Nervous, Josh hopped and shook out his tension like a sprinter at the starting line. "Mojo...mojo," he chanted.

"Kid," Blues Man said, "it ain't a race. It's music." Blues Man pulled out his harmonica and waved it, intimating that Josh do the same.

"Right...sorry." Josh took a deep breath, rubbed his sweaty palms down the sides of his pants, and withdrew his harmonica from his pocket.

Blues Man nodded to the group behind him. Music exploded as the curtain parted revealing a full house. The band got down, their funky blues shaking the bar to applause. Josh squinted into the glare of the stage lights, frozen stiff. Blues Man nodded to him encouragingly. Josh swallowed hard, took a deep breath, and within another couple of beats was playing his heart out.

At a small table near the front of the stage sat Maggie, Ms. Summers, and a very excited Becky, who was alternately pointing at Josh and chattering to Maggie and Ms. Summers. Maggie smiled, glowing with pride.

At the back of the bar, Chad Jefferson spun around on his bar stool. He grinned and pulled out a small, black notebook. His head bobbing to the music, he clicked his pen and drew a line through ~~Learn an instrument and perform it before an audience~~. Other items were similarly marked off.

Chad pocketed the notebook and watched Josh relax and begin to really enjoy himself. A moment later a bouncer strolled up to Chad and handed him Chad's camera. The bouncer was an ex-linebacker for the Green Bay Packers; a beefy, middle-aged man, out of shape—but pity the person who ever tried to find out how badly—and an old friend of Chad's.

"Thanks, Charlie," Chad said, slapping a ten in the guy's hand.

"No sweat," Charlie said. "You know, I wonder if that kid even knows who he's playing with up there."

"I doubt it," Chad said.

"How do you think he swung it?"

"Beats me. I chalk it up to what I call the humble bee theory."

Charlie chuckled. "You got a theory for everything, don't 'cha brother? The humble bee, huh? And what might that bee be?"

Chad answered, "I once read that the inventor of the Bell Helicopter was mystified by the flight of the male bumblebee. He wondered how the hell the blimpy bug could get off the ground. The bee was chubby, had itty-bitty wings, and they were in the wrong aerodynamic position to boot. And yet, the damn thing buzzed about with the greatest of ease, landing and taking off without any concern for the laws of physics. The engineer puzzled and puzzled over the ignorant little bug. It just didn't make sense. According to all the laws of aerodynamics, the male bumblebee simply should not be able to fly."

"That's funny," Charlie said, "but I guess the guy finally figured it out, huh?"

Chad nodded and sipped his beer. "Yep. The engineer concluded that the bumblebee flew because the little fella was too dang dumb to know that it couldn't."

~

"Twenty-nine," Maggie called out. "Come on Josh, one more!"

Josh struggled to get his chin over the pull-up bar. Then, all at once, his head shot upward, easily clearing it.

"Thirty!" Becky cried, her arms around his legs, giving him a boost.

"Hey," Maggie said. "That's cheating. You're going to have to do them all over again tomorrow."

Josh dropped from the bar and collapsed on the ground. "I'm gonna get you for that, Becky!" he threatened.

Becky squealed in laughter and ran off.

"Harpo," Josh commanded. "Go get her!"

The dog looked at Josh, sneezed, and went back to licking his balls.

~

Afterwards, Maggie and Becky accompanied Josh to the high school track and cheered him with each pass. Arms and legs pumping, Josh ran giving it his all. Maggie clicked the stopwatch as Josh sped by the finish line. He looked back, bent at the waist, his chest heaving. Maggie frowned and shook her head.

On the hill overlooking the track field, another stopwatch clicked the same time. Chad pulled down his binoculars and checked his stopwatch: 5:16.

Chad raised his binoculars again and saw Josh walk back towards the girls, disappointed and shaking his head. "Hang in there, Josh," he said.

~

Maggie laid Josh's arm on her lap and reached into her first-aid kit beside her on the grass. Step by step, she instructed him on how to tie a bandage. The Marx Brothers looked on in curiosity.

"See," Maggie said putting on the finishing touch, "nothing to it. Now, the only thing left to learn before you pass your first-aid certification is mouth to mouth resuscitation." She grinned and said seductively, "Ready?"

"Whenever you are," Josh said. He turned to the dogs. "Groucho, come here boy. You're up."

Maggie shoved Josh over, "Stinker!"

≈

Required to learn how to waltz, Josh turned to the Senior Center's frail-but-energetic, eighty-six year-old Betty Wilson. She claimed to have won a dance with Fred Astaire at a New York charity ball when she was young, and that the dance was "the four most blissful minutes of my life." Josh wondered, for by the third lesson the old lady spent most of the time with her head nestled on Josh's shoulder.

As Josh swept Betty up and down the checkered tiled floor, he was unaware that across the street Chad was snapping his picture through the glass window with his telephoto camera.

Chad chuckled. "Get that boy a top hat and cane."

≈

Strolling through the park Josh noticed that Maggie's shoelace had come undone. He guided her to a park bench. Maggie sat down, unsure what he was up to. Josh kneeled and began to tie the shoe on her prosthetic. Maggie squirmed, self-conscious; but Josh ignored her awkwardness.

Maggie said, "You're sexy."

"I'm tying your shoe."

"I know. I think gentlemen are sexy."

Josh chuckled, gave Maggie his hand and yanked her to her feet. They continued walking.

"Dad did the same thing for my mom. When I read his journal, I recalled a hundred little things he used to do for her. He really loved her."

Josh paused reflectively. And as he did, Maggie wondered if Josh meant something by his comment; that perhaps he was clumsily telling her that he loved her too. Was he too obtuse to know what he had just intimated?

"When Mom died," Josh continued, "he had to learn that there were some things that are not within our will, and I imagine for a guy like my dad, that must have been a tough lesson to learn."

Obtuse it is, she thought. Maggie turned to him and said, "Why have you never asked me about my leg?"

"Honestly, because I didn't know how to."

"It was trampled in a horse-riding accident when I was sixteen. Afterwards, I had to learn the same lesson as your father. I wish I hadn't been such a slow learner, but…"

"He'd have liked you a lot."

"Really?" Maggie said, pleased.

"Yeah. Definitely."

Maggie took Josh's hand in hers. "Well, I'll settle for a chip off that block, Mr. McCain."

It was a glorious spring day, and list or no list, walking hand-in-hand they felt a growing bond that transcended deadlines. No matter how things turned out, they each knew that the path they were journeying on was leading them to a place neither had dared to go before.

Maggie said, "If you hadn't helped out Becky and actually finished the list, what would you have done with all that money?"

"Of course I thought about it all the time, especially at first. It was a heck of an incentive. But weird as it sounds, I got sick of thinking about it. I really did. If I succeeded, if I had all that money, I could do anything I wanted. Only, I didn't know what I wanted. Not a clue! It was a scary revelation."

"Still, most people would love to be in such a clueless position."

"Yeah, I know."

"So what are you going to do once you pass this test?"

Josh shrugged, unconcerned. "I'll think of something."

"You don't seem very worried about it," Maggie said.

"Why should I worry? I know that if I can do this, I can do anything. It sounds glib, but I mean it. I can say along with Henry David Thoreau: 'I learned this, at least, by my experiment: that if one advances confidently in the direction of his dreams, and endeavors to live the life which he has imagined, he will meet with a success unexpected in common hours. He will put some things behind, will pass an invisible boundary; new, universal laws will begin to establish themselves around and within him; or the old laws be expanded, and he will live with the license of a higher order of beings. In proportion as he simplifies his life, the laws of the universe will appear less complex, and solitude will not be solitude, nor poverty poverty, nor weakness weakness. If you have built castles in the air, your work need not be lost; that is where they should be. Now put the foundations under them.'"

"Very good, Mr. McCain."

"Yeah, well, I wonder how long it'll be before I forget all these passages I've memorized."

Maggie said, "Maybe I shouldn't pry, but I confess I sometimes wonder why your dad stipulated that your Aunt Brooke would get the money if you failed. Why would your failure be her success? What made her so special?"

"I don't know. He rarely spoke of her to me. Dad subscribed to the maxim that if you haven't anything nice to say about someone, it's best to say nothing at all. She never believed in him, that I know. In the early years of struggle she offered only ridicule and I-told-you-so's. He ignored her scoffing and just kept plugging away."

"Then why would he leave her such a huge sum of money,

over and above the already generous amount he left her? Why not just add your surrendered portion to one or more of the many charities he supported?"

"I've wondered that, of course, but I don't know the answer."

"I do," Maggie said.

"Oh you do, do you?"

"Yes. It's simple. He did it for you."

"Oh great Sphinxtress, you're going to have to dumb it down a lot more than that for a simpleton like me."

"Your dad knew how you felt about her. He knew you better than you knew yourself, and he knew you were a full-blooded McCain. He believed that the idea of your aunt getting his hard-earned money would insult the very marrow in your bones. He thought it would spur you on, if for no other reason than to see that she wouldn't go traipsing off with it."

"Well," Josh said, "if that's the case then he was way too smart for his own good, 'cuz that's exactly what she is going to do."

"If I'm right, do you feel regret for letting her get away with it?"

"No," Josh stated flatly. "Becky is worth more than Brooke will ever be, no matter how much of my dad's money she has. Dad miscalculated. There's a first time for everyone, I guess."

"He miscalculated all right," Maggie said. "But he didn't overestimate his son; he underestimated him."

40

MESHUGANA

*J*osh walked into the Sunny Day Senior Center, and as had become his habit, the first thing he did was cast his eyes towards the garden window where Berkowitz always sat. The board was set for a game of chess, but Berkowitz wasn't there. A sinking feeling gripped Josh's stomach, and he hurried to Berkowitz's room. He dashed back out and hunted down Mrs. Johnson.

"Sandy, where's Berkowitz?"

"Oh, Josh, I'm so sorry. We wanted to call you but you don't have a phone."

"What's wrong? Where is he?"

"Mr. Berkowitz passed away in his sleep."

"What? I just saw him the other day. He looked fine. How—?"

"He was old, Josh. It was just his time. I'm really sorry. I know how much you—"

"So where is he?"

"We knew of no next of kin, so he was buried in the county cemetery."

"No service, no nothing?"

"I don't know what the procedure is exactly," she said regretfully.

"He deserved better. He was a hero. He was—" Josh turned and took off running.

"Josh!" Mrs. Johnson called after him.

"There's something I gotta do," he said, and rushed out the door.

~

Josh skidded his Schwinn to a halt outside the cast iron gate of a modest brownstone house and jogged up the walkway through the small, well-manicured lawn and garden to the doorstep. He rang the doorbell.

A pale, but otherwise handsome and healthy-looking boy of eleven wearing a yarmulke and long curly sidelocks, or *paot*, answered the door.

"Hi," Josh said, "is your dad around?"

The boy looked Josh up and down and said, "One minute." He walked off and returned shortly with an elderly man, also wearing a yarmulke and with long *paot* that meshed with his bushy, gray beard.

"Can I help you?" the man asked.

"You don't know me, but—"

"I do know you. You are the *meshugana* who runs wild down the street every morning. You knocked me over catching a bagel."

"That was you? I'm *really* sorry about that."

The man waved his hand. "It was a good catch." He smiled. "So, what brings you to my door?"

"I have a question, or maybe a request, or well…"

"Don't worry. Either the answer will be yes or no. Or maybe. Ask."

"Right. Okay. See, I have a friend. He died two days ago, almost three. He's Jewish. I don't know any Jewish people, I mean, I do, a few, but I need a rabbi. My friend had no family or relatives that I know about, and well, he was buried in the county cemetery, and he was a really great guy, a war hero, and—"

"What was his name?"

"Berkowitz."

"Did he have a first name?"

"I...I just called him Berkowitz."

"I see. And you want what exactly?"

"I just think he should get a prayer or something, whatever it is you, you know, do. He was a GI in World War II and was there when we liberated Dachau, and...I'm babbling, I know. Sorry, um, Rabbi, Sir."

"You say he had no family?"

"He mentioned once that he had a son somewhere, California, I think, but I got the impression that the son...that they weren't very close."

"So," the rabbi said, "you were like his son."

"Well, I don't know about—"

"That you have come to me for this tells me you are." The rabbi's hand shot out and tore the pocket off of Josh's white dress shirt.

"Hey! What—?"

"It's called *keriyah*. We do this as a sign of grief and mourning." The rabbi smiled. "I bet you're thinking that you wish you had worn a different shirt."

Josh nodded. "What else can we do? And does it require losing another shirt?"

"Do you know where he was laid to rest?"

Josh pulled a piece of paper from his back pocket. "Yeah, I went to the county office and they looked it up for me." He handed the paper to the old man.

The rabbi pulled a pair of bifocals from his pocket and looked at the paper. "We can find it. Meet us there this evening at six. We shall say *kaddish* for Mr. Berkowitz."

"*Kaddish*," Josh repeated. "That's a special prayer I take it."

"Very special."

"Great. I really, really appreciate it, Rabbi, Sir. Um, I don't have much money. But I can—"

"You think that the Almighty would have us charge for *kaddish*? See you at six." He rubbed Josh's head and closed the door.

Josh walked to his bike and rode back to the Senior Center. He didn't tell anyone what he had been up to. After his regular duties Josh entered Berkowitz's room and put the few possessions that belonged to the man into a box. Among the things he put aside for safekeeping were some papers, a scrapbook, a photo album, and Berkowitz's Army uniform and war medals.

41

SECOND WIND

"*W*hat did he do with the money?" Jeffrey Barnes asked.

Chad said, "A couple of days after we last saw him, I ran into Bob Hillman at the bank. He said Josh had been in to see him. He said the money was gone."

"Already?" Barnes said in disbelief. "What did he blow it on?"

"A girl," Chad answered.

"A girl?" Powers exclaimed. "All of it?"

Chad opened his hands as if mimicking an explosion. *"Poof,"* he said.

"Must be a hell of a woman," Powers said.

"Maybe one day," Chad said. "But now she's only about eight years old. It went for a kidney transplant. Bob helped him set up a trust with the rest of the money to help cover future expenses."

Brooke smirked. "Like father, like son."

"What's that supposed to mean?" Barnes snapped.

"Clearly, neither of them knew the value of money."

Thinking now the most opportune time, Chad reached into the pocket of his leather jacket and flung a stack of snapshots across the McCain Industries conference table. His little black notebook landed spinning on top of them.

Barnes, Powers, and an especially astonished Brooke, leaned closer and examined the photos: Josh doing push-ups and pull-ups, dancing, at the aikido *dojo*, teaching Kazu, performing at the blues bar with his harmonica, Maggie teaching him first aid, in a garage with a carburetor in his hand, and even a photo of Josh standing beside a grave with ten old Jewish men with a yarmulke on his head, holding a Hebrew prayer book upside down. Incomprehension on their faces, Barnes and Powers turned to Chad for an explanation.

Chad said, "All taken *after* Josh accepted the money."

"Who died?" Wayne Powers asked.

"His chess partner."

"Chad...?" Jeffrey Barnes said questioningly.

"Before you say what you're gonna say, I want you to imagine that Taylor is sitting in his chair right now." Chad nodded towards the head of the table.

Silence.

Brooke squirmed, but said nothing.

"Does Josh know about this?" Powers asked.

"Not a clue."

"But Chad," Barnes said, "he already took the money."

"Jeffrey, Taylor himself was given a second chance once, remember? You don't think he'd be willing to do the same for his son?"

Devastated by the turn of events, Brooke opened her mouth to object, but on second thought she held her tongue.

"I realize that, Chad, but Taylor gave us strict orders—"

"To do what we felt was right," Chad interrupted. "When Taylor learned he was dying he gave you, his most trusted friend, power of attorney. You always did right by the man when he was here, Jeffrey. I say it's up to you to do right once more now that he isn't."

"But he has to complete the list, right?" Barnes said.

"Absolutely. Every item on it—same deadline, and without any knowledge of this discussion."

Powers said, "Any idea what's left on the list?"

"I got some more investigating to do, but there are still some major obstacles, and his chances are slim-to-none that he can pull it off."

"So why even bother?" Powers asked.

"Because I think we should leave it up to Josh as to what he can or can't do. Something got into that boy, and we owe it to Taylor to see if it isn't a little of Taylor himself. Besides, what difference does another few weeks make?" He turned to Brooke, a sly smile on his face. "Right, Brooke?"

"It's not like I have any say in the matter, gentlemen, now is it?" she said coolly. "If you'll excuse me, you've wasted enough of my time as is."

Brooke stood, grabbed her purse and marched out the door, her perfume trailing behind her.

Chad sneezed. "Man, I swear she wears that bug spray just to piss me off."

Brooke exited the building and strode fuming down the sidewalk. She put her cell phone to her ear.

"That's right, Mr. Tweene," she said, furious. "All of it. Things were never supposed to get this far … Yes, he still must complete the list. However, since you have proven to be utterly useless, I'll be handling things from now on. But I still have a couple of jobs for you to do, including making me a key, so keep your phone close." She tapped off and pocketed her phone.

~

Josh studied the list as he brushed his teeth and readied to meet Maggie for a movie. Nearly everything on the list had been crossed off.

He still had to knit a sweater, but as a glance towards the nearly finished sweater told; that would be any day now. He ran his finger down the list and stopped at: *Hitchhike 500 miles*. Then, continuing down the list he came to: *Visit the grave of Henry David Thoreau*. And further down: *Climb Mount Katahdin*.

Josh walked over to the wall calendar. He tapped on September 14th, which was circled in red. Time was running out fast.

～

Josh stared at the clock tower outside the theater, his hands clasped in prayer. "Come on, come on…"

The clock struck eight.

He threw his arms up in victory and danced a jig, "Yes!"

Maggie tapped him on the shoulder. He spun and saw her smiling face.

"You're late!" Josh said triumphantly.

"Impossible."

He pointed to the clock tower. "It's eight o'clock. You're one minute late."

"That clock is two minutes fast," Maggie replied.

"No, it isn't."

"Yes, it is. Look…" She showed Josh her watch.

"How do I know your watch isn't slow?"

"Because it's me—Maggie the atomic clock."

"Yeah, well, you'd say about anything to prove me wrong."

"Fine. You want to bet? Twenty dollars," she said confidently.

"Um…no."

"Okay, then," Maggie said. She took his arm and they headed towards the ticket counter. "But nice try, sport."

Later, the movie in progress, an impish grin on her face, Maggie walked her fingers over Josh's legs towards his crotch. Josh slammed his hand down on top of her teasing fingers.

"You're so mean," he said.

Maggie snickered and pecked him on the cheek.

~

Chad Jefferson unlocked Josh's door and stealthily entered. He perused the room and approvingly noted the refinished floor and cabinets, and the freshly painted walls. He also noticed the poems and passages that Josh had posted about the apartment for memorization. He snapped a dozen pictures with his cell phone. Chad pulled out his notebook, clicked his pen, and drew a line through more items from the list. He pocketed the notebook and left.

In the foyer below, Brooke Sievert was about to climb the staircase when she heard footsteps. She disappeared into a utility closet across from the mailboxes a moment before Chad descended into the foyer.

Chad sniffed at the air and scrunched his nose. Back outside, he sneezed. *Who in this neighborhood could afford Eau de Pu-Pu?* He glanced back, suspicious.

Chad got into his car, drove off, and then pulled a U-turn and parked within eyeshot of Josh's apartment. He picked up his telephoto camera and aimed it towards Josh's window.

A light went on inside the apartment and he saw a silhouette inside the room. Chad smirked.

~

Whistling "Hardheaded Woman," Josh returned home and inserted his key into the door's lock. That's weird, he thought, I've never forgotten to lock the door before. In his haste to beat Maggie to the theater he must have forgotten. He flicked on the light, and froze. The ransacked apartment looked as if it had suffered a rampaging tornado.

"Oh, no…"

Josh stepped gingerly across the floor to the dresser tipped on its side, its drawers overturned beside it. He rummaged through his clothes until he located a pair of gray sweat socks.

He stuffed his hand into one of the socks and withdrew a small jewelry box. To his great relief, Berkowitz's Silver Star sat unmolested inside. He tipped the dresser back up, snapped the box closed, and then set it absently atop the dresser. His eye had spotted something else to groan about.

Josh waded through the debris to the tipped-over kitchen table, and from under it, he pulled out the badly mangled sweater. Recalling how long it had taken him to get that far, and all he had yet to do on the list, he doubted he had time to knit another. Wordless and dispirited, Josh stood amid his trashed apartment and contemplated the destruction.

"Fluffy..."

He tiptoed through the mess over to the potted rubber tree plant lying on its side. He set the plant upright, scooped up the spilled soil with his hands, and dumped it back into the pot. Josh examined the plant's leaves and removed two that had been badly crushed. He recalled the skeleton the plant had been two years earlier, and how Kyle had mocked him for wanting to keep it. Now the plant was bigger and leafier than ever.

"You've seen worse days, girl," he said.

It would take a day to clean up the mess. Time he didn't have. He wondered if the Fates had spoken. What was the point of continuing now? Josh spotted his *Butt-buster Calendar* among the wreckage. The day's page was pinned back under his copy of the Bible, revealing tomorrow's quote:

Friday, September 6
"Most people never run far enough on their first wind to find out they've got a second."
— William James (1842-1910), American Philosopher

Josh set Bible and calendar on top of the dresser, and fists to hips, he surveyed his apartment. "Screw it."

He kicked his way through the wreckage to the closet and dug out his backpack.

42

FIELD OF BEANS

*A*n old, mud-covered pickup truck with four fat hogs standing in the back stopped along the highway. The driver honked and Josh's head popped up from between the hogs. In his hands he held knitting needles and the beginning of another sweater.

Josh tossed his pack over the side, jumped out, and waved goodbye. It took him three hours to catch that lift. Noting the storm clouds on the horizon, he hoped the next ride wouldn't make him wait so long.

He slung his pack over his shoulder and put out his thumb.

～

That morning, Kazu entered his *dojo* and saw on a chair next to the light switch a picture frame and an envelope. He picked the frame up and smiled proudly.

Kazu opened the envelope and pulled out a handwritten letter:

Kazu-sensei,

As the great philosopher Spinoza said, "Everything excellent is as difficult as it is rare." You, my friend, have helped me to know such virtue when I see it.

Please accept this as a token of my gratitude for all you have done for me, and for all your excellence.

Thumbs up,

Josh

Kazu wiped away a tear and gave the envelope a shake. Out came Josh's prized Ichiro baseball card, now laminated to maintain its mint condition.

Kazu held the card up with admiration. *"Yatta!* Ichiro *da!"*

～

As Josh stood shivering in the rain with his thumb out, Maggie stood ankle deep in the jumbled debris of his apartment. Josh had informed her of the break-in and the damage the criminal had caused. She told him that he should call the police, but Josh said he didn't have time, and that time was the only thing of real value that he had lost. No, Josh insisted, first things first. He had to give the list one final effort, or else always wonder if he hadn't tried hard enough.

Maggie took it upon herself to tidy up the mess. He was on his own from here and it was the only thing she could do to help. As she cleaned she noted the books, the quotes, the poems, the magazine rejection slips, the demolished sweater, and the harmonica. She picked up the harmonica and blew a lugubrious note. "You hang in there, hero-boy."

On the dresser Maggie spotted the jewelry box. In his haste, Josh had forgotten to hide it back in the sweat sock for safekeeping. Maggie knew a jewelry box when she saw one, and her heart skipped a beat at the thought that inside was a sparkling surprise she wasn't meant to see yet.

Did she dare open it?

Sure she did, and frowned. Then Maggie noticed a note stuck to the roof of the box. She unfolded it and read:

I leave this Silver Star to my friend and chess partner Josh McCain in good faith that he will prove far more victorious in life than he was in chess.
   — Berkowitz

≈

Dawn found Josh slogging along a deserted country road. He stopped and sat down to rest, and to take in the kaleidoscopic panoply before him. After the sun stepped out of its colorful robe, he took up the sweater and knitting needles and continued to knit as fast as he could, stopping only when the rare car approached.

Three lifts and ten hours later, Josh was sauntering alongside Walden Pond: a glossy, placid lake about half a mile long; a glistening, dark jewel set in pine wooded hills of gravel and sand, covered with a leafy undergrowth of huckleberry, willow, and young shrubberies. No wonder Thoreau lived here two years, he thought.

Josh recalled his father having asked him more than once if he'd like to drive out to Walden Pond together, and how he had laughed off the suggestion. He had "better things to do." Josh sighed. What he wouldn't give for such an outing with his father now, he thought.

He rounded a bend and came upon a large stone cairn. He stopped and read the sign that marked the makeshift monument. It read:

"I went to the woods because I wished to live deliberately, to front only the essential facts of life, and see if I could not learn what it had to teach, and not, when I came to die, discover that I had not lived."
   — Thoreau

Josh set a stone on top of the cairn with the others.

Afterwards, he walked the trail from Walden to the town of Concord, home to the sage, Ralph Waldo Emerson; the mystic, Bronson Alcott, and Alcott's famous daughter and author, Louisa May Alcott; Nathaniel Hawthorne, the author of *The Scarlet Letter*; and of course, the inimitable Henry David Thoreau.

While in town he visited the Emerson House; Orchard House, where Louisa May Alcott wrote most of *Little Women*; and Hawthorne's Old Manse. Then he treated himself to a sundae at a quaint little ice cream parlor. There he wrote a postcard to Maggie as proof that he had made it to Concord.

After mailing his postcard, Josh continued on to famed Sleepy Hollow Cemetery. The list required that he visit the graves of Concord's most famous philosophers and friends, the champions of self-reliance and American exceptionalism—Ralph Waldo Emerson and Henry David Thoreau.

Josh located the tremendous, uncarved block of rose quartz that distinguished Emerson's grave. Nearby he found Thoreau's grave and the knee-high, stubby little tombstone that marked it, which read simply: *Henry*. At each grave, Josh bowed his head reverentially, gave the American giants his father's regards, and thanked them for their inspiring tours of duty. Then he shouldered his rucksack and continued on his way.

Josh spent the remainder of the afternoon roadside a few miles out of town, his back to a bean field, sitting on his pack with his thumb out. Hungry and cold, he wondered if he'd catch another ride before it got dark. He didn't, and ended up sleeping in the bean field. He dreamed about Alfonso.

Rosa set down a plate of beans and tacos in front of Maggie and Becky, asking, "Any word from Josh?"

Maggie shook her head.

Rosa said, "That boy is very strange. How do you put up with him?" As she spoke she kept a wary eye on Josh's part-time replacement at the far end of the restaurant, the same pimple-faced young man who was sitting at the counter when Josh applied for his job so many months earlier.

Maggie said, "I like strange, Rosa."

"Strange is not good, Muffie," Alfonso said from the kitchen. "We can't make *frijoles* from lima beans."

"Why not?" Becky asked.

"Ayy, Buffy," Alfonso said emerging from the kitchen. "If you make *frijoles* with lima beans then somewhere a rabbit grows a trunk."

"That's silly," Becky said. "Rabbits don't have trunks. Elephants have trunks."

"Exactly," Alfonso said.

"I don't get it," Becky said.

Alfonso nodded. "*Sí*, Buffy. Ask your Muffie."

"But I don't get it either, Al," Maggie said.

The four were startled by a loud *crash*, the sound of smashing plates. Everyone turned to the unfortunate busboy.

The young man grinned wanly and shrugged in helpless wonder, shards of shattered dishes at his feet. "Sorry," he croaked.

"Ayy, Daddy," Rosa said, "I can't wait for our lima bean to get back. Soon we will have no more dishes."

Alfonso nodded profoundly. "*Sí*, our lima bean has respect for dirty dishes."

Maggie and Becky turned to each other and giggled.

≈

The driver of the pickup truck, a middle-aged man in cowboy hat and boots, looked over at Josh who had just pulled out his sweater and begun to busily knit away.

The man arched a curious brow. "Who's that for?" he inquired.

"A friend," Josh said without looking up.

The man eyed Josh's work and shook his head. "Must not be a very good friend," he said.

Josh chuckled. "Yeah, well, hopefully he'll think it's the thought that counts."

"He?"

"It's not what you think," Josh said quickly.

"Hey, friend, to each his own."

"But—"

"Say no more, say no more," the man said, tugging on his hat brim. "Not all thoughts are in need of en'ertainin'."

Kazu's students stood admiring a handmade certificate in a handsome frame on the *dojo* wall. They took turns shaking Kazu's hand and slapping him on the back. The award read:

> This certifies that Kazuhiro Watanabe has graduated with highest honors from the Josh McCain School of English.

The truck pulled to the side of the road and Josh got out, his knitting in his hand. He waved goodbye to the cowboy, looked up and saw a large mountain looming before him, Mount Khatadin.

43

CONTACT!

*S*ore and weary from two days of hiking, Josh rounded another bend in the mountain trail. He stopped, took a slug of water from his canteen, and looked up. The summit was in sight, but it would soon be too dark to proceed. He figured he should use what little light was left to find a spot to sleep for the night.

Exhausted, Josh chose a strip of lumpy, relatively horizontal ground a few yards from the trail. Handfuls of trail mix sufficed for dinner; sleep being the nourishment he craved more than anything. Concern for cold, bugs, snakes, bears or other undesirables was no match for his fatigue, and within minutes of zipping himself up in his sleeping bag he drifted off to sleep.

Come daybreak, Josh sat on a boulder beholding the vast, woolly green below. The vista filled him with awe. A line he had memorized from the Book of Psalms fluttered up from the recesses of his mind. He spoke the words aloud: *"This is the day which the Lord has made. We will rejoice and be glad in it."*

Josh dug a dog-eared paperback from his pack—Thoreau's *Maine Woods*. He stood and read a passage from Thoreau's essay on Mount Khatadin:

"...I stand in awe of my body, this matter to which I am bound has become so strange to me. What is this Titan that has possession of me? Talk of mysteries! Think of our life in nature—daily to be shown matter, to come in contact with it—rocks, trees, wind on our cheeks! The solid earth! The actual world! Contact! Contact! Who are we? Where are we?"

Josh closed the book and sat back down on the boulder. He tucked his knees under his arms and watched the rest of the sunrise. He had one last task to complete.

The trip down Khatadin was even more arduous than the trip up. Sore and stiff, he often slipped or slid on loose dirt or a steep incline. A broken or twisted ankle was the last thing he needed now. In one fell swoop his slim chance for completing the list would become no chance. His legs quivered and his back hurt, and he wished that he could just snap his fingers and be home. But home was a long ways off, and the time he needed to get there was fast running out.

～

Maggie strolled up to the hospital receptionist, Jill Walsh, a red-headed and freckled longtime confidant of Maggie's. Maggie noted the digitally displayed clock on the wall: 9:33 p.m.

"Jill," she asked, "have there been any calls for me?"

"No. Are you expecting one?"

"Josh. He should have been back by now."

"Where is he?"

"Jersey, I hope. Page me if he calls, okay?"

"Sure thing."

～

Josh tramped wearily alongside the highway with his thumb out. A black sedan passed, then slowed and stopped. Josh didn't even notice. It took a honk of the horn to snap him from his stupor. He jogged over.

"Where ya headed?" the driver asked, a genial, middle-aged man in a baseball cap and glasses.

"Jersey."

"Would you settle for Connecticut?"

Josh's face lit up. "Are you kidding? That would be great. Long story, but I got about twenty-four hours to get home."

"Then hop on in."

Josh set his backpack in the back seat and climbed in. The man pulled back onto the highway.

"My name is Bill," he said, offering his hand. "Bill Tweene."

"Josh."

"Looks like you've been on a little adventure."

"You might say that, yeah."

"Oh youth! I sure miss those days. So, mission accomplished, as they say?"

"Not quite, but, yeah, I'm getting there."

"Good for you," Tweene said. "I like seeing young people venturing out to see what they are made of."

Mr. Tweene turned on some soft music. Josh, his worries eased, the hardest part of the trip behind him, he felt suddenly, completely, exhausted. He nestled into the comfy leather seat and began to nod off.

"Don't mind me," Tweene said. "You look beat. Go ahead and catch some winks. I'll wake you when we get there."

"Thanks," Josh said, and fell fast asleep.

The car sped through the night.

44

WANDERING KNIGHT

*J*ill shook her head, no. Maggie frowned and looked at the digital clock on the wall: 2:11 a.m.

~

Mr. Tweene noted the same time on the dashboard of his car, and slowed to a stop. He glanced over at Josh who was sound asleep and gave him a little nudge.

Groggy, Josh rubbed his eyes and tried blinking the pitch of night into something he could recognize.

Tweene said, "Sorry, but this is where we say goodbye."

"Where are we?"

Tweene pointed at an intersection of two country roads. "Catch a lift from there and that should take you all the way in. One solid lift and you'll have no trouble making your appointment."

Josh shook the man's hand and stepped out of the sedan. He grabbed his backpack from the backseat, and then stuck his head back into the car. "Thanks a lot. Sorry I wasn't much company."

"Forget it," Tweene said. "You were better company than you know."

"I snored?"

Tweene chuckled. "Something like that. Take care, son. I hope you find whatever it is you're looking for."

"Another good lift like yours and I can do the rest," Josh said confidently.

"That's the spirit!" Tweene said. He waved goodbye and drove off. He watched Josh shrink out of sight in his rearview mirror, and shook his head. "Nice try, kid. If life gave a shit, it would have given you an 'A' for effort."

Josh shouldered his pack and started walking.

An hour later he stood in the middle of an empty country road consulting a map with his flashlight. Disoriented, he looked around for some kind of marker or point of reference, but he saw none. He scratched his head in bewilderment, and continued walking.

The weathered old-timer at the two-pump gas station didn't like being awoken by Josh's pounding fist on the door. But the man's testiness didn't come close to the disbelief and shock that Josh felt when the man gave him the startling news.

Josh threw his pack to the ground and swung at the air. "Son of a—!" he said, filling the blank with a stifled primal scream. He stomped over to a pay phone next to the toilets and dialed Maggie.

"Ohio?!" Maggie exclaimed. She was standing at the hospital reception desk, the phone pressed tightly to her ear because of a lousy connection. Maggie checked the digital clock. It read: 3:58 a.m. "You can still make it, Josh! Take a bus, or, or…"

"You don't understand," Josh said, "I'm standing by a stinky bathroom at *Gabe's Gas and Garage* in nowhere U.S.A. The closest bus station is fifty miles away. Besides, I'm broke. Maggie, there's no way I'm gonna be back by sundown." Josh looked into the empty countryside. "That son of a... It's over."

"Maybe I can come out and—"

"Forget it, Maggie. There's not nearly enough time."

"But you're so close to finishing. I feel awful for you."

"We gave it our best shot. Some things just aren't within our will, you know."

"No, this isn't going to be one of them. There must be—"

"Look, I'm out of change. I gotta go. I'm sorry, Maggie. I know how much you hate it when I'm late."

"Oh, Josh…"

"I'll see you in a day or two. I love you, Maggie."

"You—?"

The phone went dead. Maggie absently handed the receiver back to Jill.

"What's wrong?" Jill asked.

"He loves me."

Jill smiled. "Bastard."

Maggie's vacant gaze came into focus on the digital clock, just as it turned from 3:59 to 4:00. Her eyes narrowed in on the four. "Ohio…?" she said cryptically. She turned to Jill with a new urgency in her voice. "Jill, I need you to look up something."

Josh tramped down the country road, his thoughts plagued by his defeat. It struck him that he had actually believed that he could do it; that had he not been the victim of some jerk's idea of a joke, he really might have managed the impossible, and completed that list. He truly had come to believe, naively or not, that if he persevered long and hard enough the "magic" Goethe said boldness contained would manifest itself. But it didn't, and he was deeply disappointed.

As he walked, Josh continued to wrestle and puzzle with the meaning of it all, for he believed that there *had* to be some meaning in it somewhere. That thought alone surprised him, and he chuckled to himself.

Two years earlier he didn't believe in anything but the satisfying of his own appetites and whimsy. And now, he thought, here he was wandering down a lonely country road like a straggling knight returning from an ill-fated search for the elusive Holy Grail, and all because one man and one woman, his father and Maggie, Arthur and Guinevere, had believed in him. *Oh, life…!*

He returned to thoughts of Maggie. She really did believe in him, and he was truly sorry he had let her down. He knew that answering his father's challenge was as important to her as to him, and he'd have loved nothing more than to prove her right. He pictured how proud and happy she'd have been; how brightly she'd have shone; and what a thrill it would have been to receive her rejoicing kiss.

Josh lifted his eyes heavenward. "Don't worry," he said. "I'm not blaming You."

He heard the approach of a car and turned to look. He stopped and put out a pleading thumb. "Come on, come on…!"

The car zoomed past and Josh threw his hands up in surrender.

He continued walking.

A minute later, over Josh's shoulder, a semi appeared on the horizon. He heard the distant, deep, hoarse blast of a horn, turned and saw the semi barreling down the highway towards him. Then, as it approached, he heard the unmistakable pitch of pressing breaks. A squeal never sounded so lovely. The semi halted beside him. Jubilant, Josh climbed in.

The semi was a late-model truck, but the cab was spacious and clean. The driver, lean and shaggy-haired, was in his late thirties, and he wore sunglasses. Both of his arms sported Navy tattoos.

"Need some company?" the man asked amiably.

"Sure do!"

The man ground the gears and drove off.

"Where ya headed?"

"Home."

The man pinched his thumbs and forefingers together over the steering wheel as if in meditation. *"H-ohhmmm,"* he chanted. He turned to Josh and smiled unabashedly. "That's my mantra, man."

Josh smiled. "Ditto, brother. *H-ohhmmm sweet h-ohhmmm!"*

The driver laughed and reached into a sack at his side. He pulled out a box of juice as Josh tugged down the sun visor to block the bright morning sun. Josh noticed a photo stuck to the vanity mirror. It was a snapshot of the driver, about 100 pounds heavier, sitting on a Harley motorcycle.

The driver ripped the straw from the side of the juice box and jabbed it into the little hole at the top. He handed the box to Josh. "Here ya go."

"Thanks, man. Pineapple, my favorite."

The man smiled. "Mine too."

Josh pointed at the picture. "That you?"

"Yep."

"Wow, how'd you lose so much weight?"

"Crash diet."

"Impressive," Josh said. He greedily slurped the juice down and stared ahead. A wave of exhaustion overtook him. His head bobbed as he tried to fight off the arms of Hypnos.

"Sleep," the man said. "I'll watch the road for you."

"The last time someone said that, when I woke up I wasn't in Connecticut anymore."

"Huh?"

"Long story. Thanks."

Josh closed his eyes and fell fast asleep. The driver reached behind the seat for a jacket and placed it over Josh. Doing so he noticed that Josh's necklace with the number 4 had inadvertently slipped out from his shirt.

The man took the 4 between his fingers and gave it a rub.

"You still got it little fella, don't ya?" He gently tucked the jacket in around Josh and grinned as his semi barreled down the highway.

～

Maggie sat alone on the fifty-yard line of the football field. She wasn't going to give up. She had left a message on Mr. Palmer's answering machine, but whether it had been received, she couldn't know, and even if it had, she didn't know if anything would or could be done about it.

And so she sat, waiting and praying, and marveling misty-eyed at the confluence of events that had brought her there. She wanted to believe that her presence at the track would act like a homing beacon, drawing Josh to her.

As further testament to her faith, she risked looking foolish by calling in reinforcements. If Josh showed up, she thought, he was going to need all the help he could get.

～

The semi pulled into a trucker rest stop and came to a halt. Josh woke up and looked around disoriented.

"Let's go," the man said.

'Where?"

"You said you were in a hurry, right?"

"Well, yeah, but…"

"Then come on," the trucker said, and jumped to the ground.

Josh shrugged, grabbed his pack and met him around the back of the semi. The man undid a latch, threw up the sliding door, and pulled down a ramp. He walked in.

Josh looked on in gawping astonishment. Then came the deep *vroom-vroom* revving of an engine. A moment later the man shot down the ramp on a Harley Davidson. He zipped once around the parking lot and pulled up skidding alongside Josh. He tossed Josh a helmet and then hit the stereo and blasted Step-penwolf's classic "Born to be Wild."

Josh hopped on, and they screeched away, Steppenwolf in their wake:

> *"Get your motor running, head out on the highway,*
> *lookin' for adventure, in whatever comes our way…"*

Josh held on for dear life as they flew down the highway weaving in and out of traffic.

> *"…here and God are gonna' make it happen, take the*
> *world in a love embrace, fire all of your guns at once*
> *and explode into space…"*

The road blurred below their feet. To Josh it looked like a river of liquid asphalt. One false move, he thought, and the river would churn him into an unrecognizable clump of clay. He squeezed the man tighter, his knuckles white with terror.

Finally, a hundred nerve-wracked miles later, the man pointed ahead towards a sign: Welcome to New Jersey. He shouted over his shoulder to Josh, "There she blows!"

45

PHAT LADY

*M*aggie looked up, and smiled. Walking towards her were her reinforcements—Kyle, Shelly, Alfonso, Rosa, Ms. Summers, Becky, Kazu, and Josh's fellow aikido students. Maggie jumped to her feet and waved to them. The group waved back and shouted greetings.

Maggie had her cheer squad, but if her champion didn't show in the next five minutes she'd have a lot of explaining to do.

Chad Jefferson put down his binoculars. Jeffrey Barnes, Wayne Powers, and Brooke Sievert turned questioningly to Chad.

"Who the hell are they?" Barnes asked.

Chad smiled. "You might say, family."

"Do they know about the money?"

"Nope," Chad said, re-raising his binoculars. "Not a clue."

"Well, Brooke," Powers said, nodding towards the setting sun, "in another five minutes you may be the wealthiest woman in town."

"Yes, well, thank you, gentlemen," she replied, hiding her glee, "but the fat lady hasn't sung yet."

Just then they heard the distant, low rumble of a motorcycle engine. It grew louder.

"What's that?" Brooke said.

They all put up their binoculars.

"Mm-hmm…" Chad hummed. "Now, that's *phat!*"

"No," Brooke mumbled. "No, no, no…"

The Harley streaked into the football stadium. It zoomed around the track, and onto the field over to Maggie and the others. Josh hopped off as his friends cheered and circled him.

"What are you all doing here?" Josh said, amazed.

Kyle said, "Maggie told us you might need some cheerleaders."

"Josh," Rosa said, "why you don't tell us you train for Olympics?"

"What?" Josh laughed. "I'm not—"

"Ayy, Jozy," Alfonso said, "no respect for fans."

Josh turned to Maggie for an explanation. "Maggie…?"

"Later," she said, stuffing Josh's shorts and running shoes into his arms. "Now quick, there's no time to waste."

Josh noticed his ride readying to leave. "Just a sec," he told her, and turned to the man. "Hey, stick around. I'll buy you a beer or something."

"Thanks," the man replied, "but I have other deliveries to make." He glanced at Maggie, winked, and pulled down the visor on his helmet.

Puzzled, Josh cocked his head at Maggie, who smiled. He turned back to the man and put out his hand. "I owe you big time."

"No, you don't."

"I sure do. Got a name? I'm gonna look you up, I promise."

The man revved his engine and started to pull away. He cast a look over his shoulder. "Call me Ishmael," he answered, and shot off.

The setting sun flashed against his license plate: Moby 4.

Josh turned to Maggie, stunned; the realization finally having hit him. "Maggie, do you know who that was?" he said excitedly. "That was Mummy Man!"

Kyle burst out laughing. "Who?"

"Hurry, Josh," Maggie said urgently. "The sun's going down."

Josh kicked off his boots and quickly changed into shorts and running shoes.

From the wooded hill above, the onlookers watched Josh do some quick stretches and then stroll resolutely to the track's faded white chalk line.

Chad readied his stopwatch. "Okay, kid," he said. "Here we go."

Maggie readied her stopwatch.

Josh gave himself one last loosening hop and got into the starting position. "Here we go," he said to himself.

Maggie held the watch in her left hand, and pointed her right into the air like a gun.

"Ready...*bang!*" She clicked her watch and Josh was off.

Binoculars raised, Chad and the others looked on nervously. The men could barely control their own legs from running in place. Brooke didn't move a muscle. Incensed, she squinted through her binoculars and grit her teeth.

Josh had four laps to run. Halfway through the first lap he was already breathing hard. He compared in his mind how he felt to other attempts he had made. He knew he was low on juice. He ignored the comparison and fought the machine. Run, he thought. *Just run.*

Chad looked tensely on. Through his binoculars he saw Josh rounding a corner of the track. One lap down and three to go. He checked his stopwatch and raised the binoculars again. "Pick it up, Josh," he said, concerned. "Pick it up."

Brooke slid him a sneering, spiteful glance.

Josh felt his lungs burn, as if the air he was sucking in was laced with napalm. His body wasn't answering the call and he knew it. He sprinted around another corner as his friends cheered him on, but their voices were distant and muffled, overpowered by his panting and the distracting, battling voices in his head.

Chad zoomed in on Josh's straining face. He checked his watch: 2:48. He frowned. "Pump, Josh. Pump!"

Josh's rhythmic breathing deteriorated into gasping gulps for air, and his legs felt rubbery and unresponsive. His heart seemed to sputter more than pound, unable to harmoniously meet the demands of his greedy lungs. He was running on blind guts now; straining, striving intestinal fortitude. His arms and legs groping for traction, he rounded another corner.

Ahead, Maggie hopped up and down, whipping her arm around like a windmill. As Josh sped past her she saw the agony-laced determination on his face. She shouted words of encouragement, but she feared the worst. Josh looked tired, and he still had a lap to go. *Did he come all this distance over the past two years just to be beat by a few ticks of a stupid stopwatch?*

Maggie knew that if he failed this final test it wouldn't lessen her admiration for him one iota. But she also knew that his disappointment would be inconsolable, and that to his mind he would always feel that he had let down both himself and his father.

Chad checked his stopwatch ... lifted the binoculars ... stopwatch ... binoculars. "Come on, Josh," he said. "Faster!"

Brooke snatched Chad's wrist and checked the stopwatch. She smirked. That lovely chalet in the south of France she had been dreaming about was only a minute away.

46
———

THE WELL

*J*osh rounded another bend. He felt himself fading. He gritted his teeth and shook off the fear.

'You can do this,' came a voice. *'Joshua, you can do this. Dig. Dig.'*

And he felt himself digging: digging, burrowing, tunneling deeper and deeper within his being. He dropped his heart like a bucket into a deep well; a secret well within him—one filled with bubbling energy and life. The bucket splashed into a reservoir of liquid light. The glistening waters rushed over the bucket's lip, filling it with silvery brilliance. He hauled up the sacred waters, and imbibed them through every molecule of his being.

The voice returned, confident and commanding. *'Now run. Run, my son, run.'*

Josh ran. His arms, legs, and breathing regained their rhythm. His strides lengthened; his breaths deepened. He felt like a cheetah, sleek and powerful and fast. He ran.

"Yeah, baby!" Chad exclaimed. "Look at him go!"

"It's like he's turned into a cheetah or something," Barnes said.

Powers said, "I guess you call that a second wind."

"That's no second wind," Chad said. "That's a hurricane!"

Chad lowered his binoculars and saw that Josh had half a lap to go. He held the stopwatch ready, but couldn't bear to look at it.

Chad, Powers, and Barnes began to chant in unison. "Go Josh go…Go Josh go…!"

Brooke glared at the men and cursed them under her breath.

Josh sprinted around the final corner, determination etched into his sweating face.

He saw the finish line in front of him. The sight of it called forth the final ounces of his enriched will. Nothing mattered more to him than crossing that line and bringing to victorious conclusion the two years he spent training to get there. He would die trying if he had to. His pounding heart and heaving breaths were of no consequence. He'd give it everything he had; there would be no regrets.

His friends huddled beside the finish line, waiting and cheering.

Josh closed in upon the final yards. In his mind's eye, he hurled his heart down the track. His body in tow, it flung forward to catch up. He dashed past the group.

Maggie clicked her stopwatch and her friends turned to her in nervous expectation.

Josh downshifted and drifted in a stumbling wobble to the grassy field. He folded at the waist, trying desperately to catch his breath, and then dropped to his knees.

Through their binoculars the onlookers saw Josh kneeling, panting like a cheetah after a lengthy and unsuccessful chase. He collapsed backwards, his arms outstretched. They lowered their binoculars and turned to Chad, their eyes fixed on the clenched hand that held his stopwatch.

Chad slowly opened his fist, sliding an anxious, squinted eye toward the watch. Hesitantly, he opened one eye, then the other. The stopwatch read: 4:58.

Josh's cheering friends swarmed him. Tears of joy trickled down Maggie's cheeks. Beside her, Becky squealed in excitement and hopped up and down and clapped her hands.

Maggie took Becky's hand and squeezed through the jubilant circle. She threw her arms around Josh and kissed him.

"You did it, Josh!" she cried. "You did it! I knew you would!"

Maggie reached into her pocket and pulled out a ribbon necklace. Hanging from it was Berkowitz's Silver Star. She placed it around Josh's neck and kissed him again. "Berkowitz knew it too," she said.

"Look, Mommy," Alfonso said proudly. "Our two lima beans are going to be in love."

"*Sí*, Daddy," Rosa said, blowing into a handkerchief. "*Gracias a Díos*. It's about time."

"*Yata!*" Kazu shouted in Japanese. He and his students scooped Josh up and hoisted him over their heads. Josh's beaming smile filled the sky.

"Hot damn, Josh," Kyle said, flicking away a tear. "Hot damn."

Sitting on the roof of the high school gym, Mummy Man smiled proudly. "Mm-mph," he said. "Mm-mph."

On the hill, Chad, Barnes, and Powers hopped up and down like school kids, patting one another on the back. Brooke stared at the ground in devastated disbelief.

She turned to the three friends, sparks flying from her eyes. "You can't do this!"

"Sure we can, Brooke," Wayne Powers said, unruffled.

"No. No, you cannot. My brother's money belongs to me. It's mine!"

"Sorry, Brooke. It's three against one, and you knew the deal."

"No, this was not the original deal. He forfeited his chance when he took the money. It's mine. Besides, he didn't finish the list."

Chad withdrew his notebook. "He did. I have it all right here."

"No, you don't," Brooke said. "He was supposed to knit a sweater, was he not? Where's your proof of that?"

"It's finished," Chad said. "I've seen it."

"Liar. That's impossible because—"

"Because what?" Chad prompted.

Wayne Powers, binoculars to his eyes, interrupted the spat with a clearing of his throat. "You might want to see this, Brooke."

Below, Josh dug into his backpack and pulled out the sweater he had been working on. He turned to Kyle.

"Blue, right?" He tossed Kyle the sweater. "Happy birthday, buddy."

Kyle held up the deformed and lopsided sweater. "Who am I?" he said. "Yoda?"

The three men turned to Brooke, folded arms across their chests and smirking grins on their faces.

Powers said, "Get over it, Brooke. You lost."

"I don't lose. I'm going to sue your ass, all of your asses!"

Chad and Powers gladly handed the stage to Jeffrey Barnes. Barnes stepped up smiling, a man in his element.

"Those are fighting words, Brooke," Barnes said.

"You're not so tough. You're all a bunch of sentimental twerps. I'll sue all right, and my New York lawyers will cut you namby-pambies to threads."

Barnes reached into his shirt pocket. "Yes, well, let me draw you a picture, Brooke. Better yet, let me show you some. *En garde.*"

He spread open Chad's time-stamped snapshots like a hand-held fan. The photos showed Brooke in front of Josh's apartment, her silhouette in his window, her license plate, Brooke leaving Josh's apartment building, and her handiwork, including the sweater she had demolished.

Barnes closed the fan and slid the snapshots back into his shirt pocket like a sword into its scabbard. He bounced his eyebrows.

Brooke quaked with astonishment and outrage. "How—?"

Chad smiled in deep satisfaction and said, "*Eau de Pu-Pu*, Brooke. I caught you hiding in the utility closet in the apartment's foyer. I smelled your bug spray, and it nailed you."

47

WAITING LIST

a towel around his waist, Josh stood freshly showered and bare-chested in front of his bathroom's steamed-up mirror. He turned to the list beside the mirror and drew the final line: ~~Run a mile under 5 minutes~~. He rubbed a circle out of the foggy mirror and smiled proudly.

Josh glanced again at the wall, smirked, and tore away the list. He weighed it thoughtfully in his hand, and then he crumpled it into a ball and fired it at the wastebasket. Two points.

He combed back his shaggy hair with his fingers and opened the door to see what Maggie was up to. To his surprise and delight, she was horizontal, lying in his bed, the sheet up to her chin. If hearts could fly, Josh's would have been doing loop-the-loops.

"It's about time," Maggie groused.

"Sorry…"

"Mr. McCain," Maggie began scoldingly. Then, unable to keep up the charade, she broke into a luscious smile. "…some things are worth waiting for." She patted the bed beside her.

Elated, Josh whipped away his towel, flinging it to Maggie, who laughed and reached her bare arms out to catch it. "Oh my," she purred.

Josh dove into bed beside her. Maggie wrapped her arms around Josh and kissed him. Josh's hand slipped under the sheet.

His explorations screeched to a halt, and an expression of confusion replaced his smile. Josh pinched the sheet between his thumb and forefinger and peeked underneath.

"Hey," he said, stumped.

"Yes…?"

"You're not…"

"Naked?"

Josh nodded dumbly.

"Actually," Maggie said, businesslike, "there's something I want to discuss with you."

"Uh-oh…"

Maggie pulled a sheet of paper from under the pillow and waved it in front of Josh's eyes. "Look familiar?"

"How did you—?"

"When I was cleaning your apartment."

"Oh…right," he said. "Drat me."

"I'm wondering how serious you are about following through with this, Mr. McCain."

"Pretty serious?"

"Not good enough."

"Pretty darn serious?"

"Mm-hmm," Maggie said, unconvinced.

"I can hardly wait to begin."

"Well, let's see, what do we have here…?" Maggie cleared her throat and began to read from the sheet of paper:

"Josh McCain's next two years. You will: Run a marathon. Become fluent in Spanish and begin learning Japanese. Visit Japan with Kazu and Keiko. Take Becky to Disneyland. Do 150 Hindu push-ups in a row, 500 Hindu squats, 50 pull-ups, and 200 leg raises and sit-ups. You will get your black belt in aikido. Go fly-fishing with Mr. Hillman. Continue volunteering at the Senior Center, and take Brooke to Saul's Deli. You will ride a bicycle across America. Look up Mummy Man. Read twenty-five classics. Knit a shawl for Ms. Summers. Buy Mick that beer, and beat Candy in pool. You will take Ms. Wilson ballroom dancing. Find Berkowitz's son, and give him his father's medals. You will memorize twenty new poems or passages. Continue studying the harmonica and cut a CD with Blues Man and his band. You will publish an Alfonso Cookbook, and with the help of Jeffrey, Wayne, and Chad, begin a book about your father's life and work. And finally, coming in dead last at number twenty-five, you will…marry Maggie Ardor?"

"Umm…"

Maggie glared at him. "*Last?*"

"Not necessarily in that order!"

The End

A MESSAGE FROM BENJAMIN LASKIN

Thank you for reading *The Will*. I hope that you enjoyed it. I recognize that there are a lot of terrific authors out there yearning for your attention, so I really appreciate that you gave one of my books a chance.

If you liked *The Will*, I hope you'll consider posting a comment at Amazon.com. Your reading experience could be valuable to those considering giving one of my novels a try, and so really make a difference. Thank you very much!

If you would like to contact me directly, I'd love to hear from you. You can email me at benjamin@benjaminlaskin.com, or reach me via my Facebook author's page, or through my website: www.benjaminlaskin.com. You can also sign up for my newsletter for the latest in news, updates, and pay no more than 99¢ for any new Ebook release.

With gratitude,
Benjamin Laskin

OTHER NOVELS BY BENJAMIN LASKIN

Did you enjoy *The Will?* There is more where that came from. All of Benjamin Laskin's novels are available both as paperbacks and e-books at Amazon.com.

Novels by Benjamin Laskin

Stormer's Pass
Say Uncle
The Will
Shooting Eros
Murphy's Luck
The Amazing Adventures of 4¢ Ned (Coinworld Series)

The Amazing Adventures of 4¢ Ned Series Coinworld Series

Coinworld: Book One
Coinworld: Book Two
Coinworld: Book Three
Coinworld: Book Four (coming soon!)

∾

STORMER'S PASS

If you can't wait for a hero, you must become one.

The sleepy town of Pinecrest is jolted from its slumbers by two unlikely citizens—star high school quarterback, Max Stormer, and Aidos, an extraordinary girl who has been living for years unobserved on the outskirts of town.

When Max is just one season away from a state championship and its accompanying rewards, the mysterious Aidos saunters out of the surrounding hills, and punts all of his plans.

Inspired by Aidos' bewitching genius, Max is soon on a collision course with those who fear the changes the remarkable girl is having on him and his friends. With a championship, scholarships, and many reputations at stake, Max finds himself leading his friends into a contest far more dangerous than a football game. Whether maverick or hero, outlaw or savior, being a champion was never harder.

Stormer's Pass is an enthralling adventure about two peoples' uncommon faith in each other, their friends, and in the miracle-making powers of courage.

～

SAY UNCLE

Believing in himself was difficult.
Someone else believing in him was deadly.

Five years have passed since the headline-exploding events in *Stormer's Pass*. For help in protecting their secrets and very lives, Max and Aidos turn to a lonely laggard named, Guy.

Guy Andrews has spent his twenty years on his back crying uncle. His hope for change arrives in the form of a beguiling young woman who recruits him to track down a man he has never met, whose name he cannot know, and whose amazing life Guy can unravel only through clues left in the man's secret-saturated past.

Lured into a world of gorgeous spies and ruthless assassins, Guy needs to find Anonymous Man before the man's many enemies find Guy. To do so, Guy must slay the slacker within, draw on wits and courage he didn't know he possessed, and solve the mystery of his own past before everyone he loves becomes its next victims.

Say Uncle is the story of a young man's humorous and inspiring struggle to find in anonymity his own unique place, and so—to say uncle no more.

∾

THE WILL

Putting the will in willpower.

Josh McCain has two years to reinvent himself. Stripped of everything that made life a swanky, booze and babe-filled breeze, Josh embarks on a grueling and often hilarious two-year regimen of self-discipline that targets his mind, body, and spirit.

Along the way, skeptics mock him; his own past taunts him; and saboteurs resolve to stop him. But Josh is determined to complete his "bucket list from hell," and prove that who he was is not as important as who he can become.

Operating in unfamiliar territory, Josh turns to a cast of quirky characters to aid him on his secret journey; persons he'd have previously shunned. Upbeat and inspiring, *The Will* is an enthralling story of goofs and grit, of the regenerative power of friendship—and if Josh doesn't blow it—real love.

∾

SHOOTING EROS

Love's greatest champion has just become evil's fiercest foe.

Trained in Heaven by secret sages; dismayed on Earth by evil men: a banished cupid commando battles to save both from a loveless oblivion.

In the year 2034, Heaven's most lethal cupid commando, Captain Cyrus, is exiled to Earth where he is expected to die a quick and unlamented death. Instead, Cyrus sets out to remind both battered and faithless worlds that some things are still worth fighting for.

Two worlds divided; one holy mission. A match made in Heaven; a love forged on Earth. Love is a battlefield.

A genre-bending epic fantasy.

~

MURPHY'S LUCK

Sometimes rotten luck is better than no luck at all.

Jinxed from birth with astonishing bad luck, Murphy Drummer hasn't ventured beyond his backyard since he was a little boy. To remedy his loneliness he immersed himself in the mastering of hundreds of hobbies, and in the process developed some amazing abilities.

Now grown up, Murphy must seek a new sanctuary where the world might be safe from his mystifying jinx. Trailing both miracles and mayhem wherever he goes, Murphy stumbles into Joy Daley, a happy-go-lucky optimist who never forgot to thank her lucky stars. The comical, topsy-turvy effects from the collision of Lady Luck and Murphy's Jinx whimsically upends the lives of everyone in their paths.

At first, Murphy's victims question who he is; at last, they'll be questioning who they aren't. An inspiring and magical romantic comedy of wood-tapping proportions.

≈

THE AMAZING ADVENTURES OF 4¢ NED (COINWORLD SERIES)

Big worlds come in coin-size packages.

In a world ruled by money, a lone 1938 nickel stands a penny short. Minus a cent, but having discovered within him a million bucks of fantastic, Ned Nickel sallies forth to save Coinworld from a worthless future.

Shunned by his fellow coins, but sought after by dogged collectors, 4¢ Ned learns that he has a most daunting destiny. With the help of a sagacious Indian nickel and a shabby and luckless Lincoln wheat penny, Ned becomes "The Four," champion of small change everywhere.

Ned must navigate the ever-changing currents of commerce as he battles for justice and searches for the love of his life, a 1922 Peace Dollar named Franny.

Beginning in 1949, Ned and his team of Raider Special Forces roll frolicking forward through the years in their attempt to save Coinworld—and perhaps the entire universe—from a valueless future.

The Amazing Adventures of 4¢ Ned is e pluribus awesome.

SPECIAL OFFER

Sign up for the Benjamin Laskin Newsletter and never pay more than 99¢ for any of my future Ebooks!

Prior to the official launch of a new book, I will email you of your chance to get the Ebook version for just 99¢ on Amazon. The secret release will be known only to subscribers before going to the book's normal price. (I only send out a few emails a year, so you needn't worry about getting bombarded with mail. I hate that as much as you do.) You also have my word that I will *never* share your email with any other individual or list. That's a promise!

Click here, or access the brief sign-up form from my website or author Facebook page.

Thank you!

ACKNOWLEDGMENTS

Great thanks and appreciation to Cheryl van Varseveld and Ingrid Snydal, Brian the Swiss Army Knife of friends, Eve H., and everyone else who provided important input and contributions, wittingly or not, during the early stages of this book.

ABOUT THE AUTHOR

Benjamin Laskin grew up in Phoenix, Arizona. He has traveled extensively and lived in a number of countries, including many years in Hamamatsu, Japan. He can now be found sauntering through the maze of narrow, stony alleyways in the ancient and legend-rich town of Safed, in Israel's upper Galilee. He is currently at work on his next novel.

Benjamin would be thrilled to hear from you. You can email him at: benjamin@benjaminlaskin.com. Or, you can contact him via his Facebook author's page, or through his website at: www.benjaminlaskin.com.

For more information or to contact Benjamin Laskin:

www.benjaminlaskin.com
benjamin@benjaminlaskin.com

49631106R00135

Made in the USA
Middletown, DE
23 October 2017